W9-AYE-921

ELISSA'S QUEST

PHOENIX RISING
1

ELISSA'S QUEST

ERICA VERRILLO

Random House New York

Text copyright © 2007 by Erica Verrillo
Jacket illustration and frontispiece map copyright © 2007 by Omar Rayyan

Published in the United States by Random House Children's Books,
a division of Random House, Inc., New York.

RANDOM HOUSE and colophon are registered trademarks of Random House, Inc.

www.randomhouse.com/kids

Educators and librarians, for a variety of teaching tools, visit us at
www.randomhouse.com/teachers

Library of Congress Cataloging-in-Publication Data
Verrillo, Erica F.
Elissa's quest / by Erica Verrillo. — 1st ed.   p.   cm. — (Phoenix rising trilogy ; bk. 1)
SUMMARY: Thirteen-year-old Elissa knows nothing of her origins until her father comes and takes her to the Citadel of the evil Khan, in exchange for soldiers to protect the kingdom that will one day be hers, but upon discovering her power, she chooses to follow her own destiny.
ISBN-13: 978-0-375-83946-7 (trade) — ISBN-13: 978-0-375-93946-4 (lib. bdg.) —
ISBN-13: 978-0-375-83947-4 (pbk.)
[1. Magic—Fiction. 2. Human-animal communication—Fiction.
3. Healers—Fiction. 4. Fathers and daughters—Fiction. 5. Fantasy.]
I. Title. II. Series: Verrillo, Erica F. Phoenix rising trilogy ; bk. 1.

PZ7.V61315El 2007   [Fic]—dc22   2006014436

Printed in the United States of America

10 9 8 7 6 5 4 3 2 1

First Edition

For my daughter, Maya

Contents

WESTERN REACH

NORTHER

Leonne

Citadel of the Khan

High
Steppes

Wilderness

SOUTHERN DESERT

Great Oasis

Alhamazar

Elissa's World

ELISSA'S QUEST

Prologue

The Ancient One sat huddled beside her fire, poking at the last faintly glowing embers with a crooked stick.

"I am so old," she grumbled.

It was true. She was indeed quite old—so old that when she calculated her age, it was not in years but in eons. How many centuries had passed since her fire had last burned bright? She had lost track. But what did it matter? Her vitality, her beauty, her brightness had faded ages ago, leaving this empty, withered husk in its place. No one remembered who she was, who she had been. She could hardly remember herself.

"Feh," she said, throwing the stick into the fire. It blazed luminous against the coals but soon burned itself out. "I'll never get it hot enough at this rate."

There was something she needed to do. Something urgent. But she was so tired. It was easier to doze, and to dream; she dreamt of the Fire—its flames rising high, consuming her with their intense heat. The Ancient One saw herself falling, burning, then rising up effortlessly, the living embodiment of light and life, her youth and beauty restored. Then the vision faded, her purpose waning along with it, like the dying embers of her fire.

Perhaps she should get up, look for kindling. But movement had become so difficult. She felt as if every part of her body were turning to stone, and each breath she took might be her last. Like an old, neglected clock, she was winding down. She was dimly aware that when she arrived at her final *tick, tock, tick . . .* everything else would come to a halt as well. At times such as these, she wasn't sure she cared. She dozed briefly and imagined the world slowing with her, stopping in its circular track—turning into a cold, dark lump of clay. Ending.

Being one with the universe has its disadvantages, she thought. *There are simply too many responsibilities.*

A spark flew from the hearth and onto the hem of her fraying robe. It glowed there for a moment, leaving only a little puff of smoke behind when it winked out. The Ancient One sniffed at the acrid smell of burning wool, so much like the smell of burning hair—or feathers. Then her eyes flew open. She remembered what she needed to do. The *Fire* must be lit! But not in this little hearth. No, what she needed was a bolt of lightning, a tempest to fan it into an inferno, and then a torrent to douse it when it had done its job. Then the Phoenix would rise once again and fly into the stars.

An ember popped, reminding her that time was running out.

The Ancient One forced herself to stand, a painstaking act completed in many small increments. She looked about, feeling the cooling draft of the hearth, the darkness, the hollowness in her bones.

"I hope it's not too late," she said.

❧ 1 ❧

On Top of the World

Far to the north, where the rim of the world meets the sky, there is a beautiful green valley. Like an upturned palm, the valley rests comfortably between the flanks of two mountain ranges, which serve to protect it from both the fickleness of Nature and the fortunes of Man. It is a timeless place, where plummeting waterfalls are transformed by the sun into rainbows, and where the moss-rimmed secrets of ancient stones remain undisturbed by the tramp of soldiers' boots. Sweet pine forests cover the lower sides of the steep mountains that shelter the valley as much from the fierce, dry winds that blow from the west as from the political tempests of the east. The valley has a name. But the people who live there simply call it "the valley," for they find no need to name a place they will never leave. Names are for strangers—traders and wanderers who pass through, and who, when they leave, take the name High Crossing away with them to share for an evening or two over a pint of ale, then discard.

Among the valley's inhabitants there was one who would take the name High Crossing and carry it with her around the world. At this moment she sat high above the valley on a blunt outcropping of granite, a crown encircling her head. The girl held quite still, hugging a brown cloak protectively around her knees, gazing out across the open fields and orchards that quilted the valley floor. Tiny stone cottages dotted the valley like scattered toys, punctuating the orderly lines of farmlands. She had lived all her life in High Crossing, but as she surveyed her small kingdom, she was the queen of all creation. Beneath her, the valley sparkled in the sun like a jewel. But beyond that shallow emerald bowl, the steady ranks of mountains stretched forever—until they disappeared into the thin silver line of the sea.

A butterfly, lazily drifting on the wind,

alighted for a moment on the girl's foot. She regarded its brightly painted wings, gently opening and closing in the sunlight, and waggled her foot playfully.

"Someday," she said, mock serious, "this will all be yours."

The butterfly floated away, uninterested in the prospect of its future inheritance. A robin hopping through the meadow behind her cocked its head. It was listening for the sound of dinner crawling through the dirt. Aside from the wind rustling through the tall grass, the world was silent—at peace.

The sun darted behind a cloud, and the moment passed. The girl stretched, and leaned over to look down toward the rocky path that led first to her gray-nosed donkey and then home. It was late, but she was not quite ready to leave. As she flung her cloak over her shoulders, Elissa, Queen of Creation, was transformed back into a humble peasant girl—her feet bare, and her disheveled hair crowned with a circlet of wilting daisies. Elissa smiled. Her kingdom was lost, but only until the next time Nana sent her on a quest to the mountains. And there was sure to be a next time. Nana was always sending her out for something, being too old to get many places herself.

Nana often sent her up to the high meadow to pick herbs and flowers. Elissa couldn't complain. Meadowsweet and rue, wild thyme and tansy, goldenrod and bee balm made for fragrant pickings, and the meadow—a riot of colors in midsummer—was irresistible. More often than not, Elissa found herself rolling in the tall grass among nodding paintbrushes and daisies, or staring transfixed into the delicate face of a violet. And lying on her back, gazing into an azure sky so deep and so clear you could almost see the wink of a star if you looked hard enough, Elissa sometimes felt as if she could simply float away. Up in the meadow, sitting on top of the world, there were no limits, no end to possibilities. Elissa was glad that this chore belonged to her alone.

Nana said Elissa had the right hands for the job. "Cool hands make a strong healer," Nana always said. Hot hands robbed the herbs of their power. Elissa held her palms against her cheeks. Contrary to Nana's claim, her hands felt quite warm. She looked down at her toes, turning her grass-stained foot first one way and then another.

Good feet, thought Elissa. *I have good, strong peasant feet.* With their straight toes and high arches, Elissa considered her feet to be her best feature. But they were merely the only feature she had an unbiased view of, mirrors being scarce in the valley. If she could see her own reflection, she would observe a girl with a candid, open face surrounded by a mass of russet hair, which, when struck by the sun, shone like a copper coin. Her brow was high and her jaw firm, indicating that here was a girl who knew her own mind, even if she did not always choose to speak it. At first glance there was nothing noteworthy about her. She was not vivacious or witty enough to attract attention. Nor did she want it. Indeed, she was so quiet that, at times, she seemed to blend in with her surroundings, like a fawn in the brush. If not for her eyes, most people would hardly have noticed her. Elissa's eyes were a brilliant emerald green, without flecks of brown or gray. They were the color of leaves when they first unfurl in the spring. No one else in the valley had eyes like hers. They cast a glow as if lit from within—a feature that made them attractive to moths at the end of the day.

Today the valley floor perfectly matched Elissa's eyes. *Harvests should be better this year,* she thought. Last year, between drought and an early frost, there had been no harvest for many of the valley's farmers. The annual summer fair, an event that normally drew traders from far and wide, had been a dismal affair. Nobody could afford the rare furs and talismans offered by the Northern tribesmen, or the spices brought from the South, much less silks from Castlemar. In fact, so many farmers had been unable to pay their crop tax that the Lord of High Crossing had declared an amnesty. Lord Bruno was a kind man and one of the valley's own, which meant he was more likely to be found breaking bread with plowmen and milkmaids than supping from gilded plates. Bruno was a man who liked to use his strength. During the fine months of summer he might be found leading a team of oxen or felling a tree. And he never exerted his right as lord and as rightful master of the valley to displace freemen from their lands when they could not pay their taxes. A farmer's pride lay in the furrows he had plowed, as had his father and grandfathers before him. Bruno knew that nothing was more disgraceful for a valley farmer than to become a landless peon.

"Get on with your business," he would tell them. "I've got enough land of my own without throwing hardworking men to the dogs. You'll pay when you've brought in a harvest." Even with their obligations forgiven, there was hunger when the harvests were poor. Lady Hilde had opened up her larder on more than one occasion this past winter, inviting dozens of people to come share bread in the sprawling Manor house at the center of the valley. And when there were too many to feed, Bruno opened up the granary so that people might take what grain they needed. Bruno knew it was the solemn duty of the lord to feed his tenants during famine.

The goatherds had not suffered as much as the farmers had, since the high mountain meadows were always dew-drenched by passing clouds that snagged themselves upon the high peaks. The goatherds blew their pipes and danced as they followed their goats into the mountains, full of good cheer. Fortunately, the goatherds were in lower pastures today, and nobody save a butterfly and an occasional robin would find Elissa as she idled the afternoon away.

Elissa's was a busy life, one in which leisure was a rare treat. At the cottage she would be kept in a state of constant motion—binding the stalks of wildflowers and herbs together, hanging them upside down to dry, sorting through roots, twigs, and crumbling leaves. Nothing was more time-consuming than turning a flower into a medicine. And when she wasn't preparing Nana's plants, she would be feeding the chickens, gathering eggs, tending the fire, and stirring the pots from which Nana made her potions and tinctures. In spite of the fact that she was supposed to be Nana's apprentice, Elissa had only the barest idea of how she made her potions. She knew which herbs went into them, but how did Nana decide how much? And in what order? Day after day she'd watch as Nana stirred the pots that bubbled in her circular hearth. Nana would throw in a handful of one herb, then a handful of another, only to shake her head after a moment or two and throw in a pinch of this or drop of that. Elissa observed her with an eagle eye, trying to understand the secret of her combinations, but it was different every time. To her questions, Nana would only reply, "You just have to do it until it's right!" Nana wasn't keen on explanations, which is probably why Elissa knew nothing about her family.

In the valley everyone knew who their relatives were. Even the smallest children could recite their family histories as far back as their grandparents' memories could stretch, which was a long way. And if their grandparents couldn't remember who was who, there was a host of other relatives who could. Valley families had lived there for so long that most were related to one another. Simply put, there was no such thing as not knowing where or how you belonged, because everybody knew. Except Elissa.

Elissa was known simply as "the orphan." She was not the only valley child who had lost both parents; she was merely the only one who did not know her parents' names, or, for that matter, the name of a single other relative. Other children who had lost their parents still had brothers, sisters, aunts, uncles, cousins. Elissa had no one. Valley dwellers, not knowing what to do with such a person, or how to treat her, ignored her. They were not cruel, or even indifferent. They simply had no way of incorporating a lone individual into valley life. The fact that she was Nana's apprentice didn't help matters, for while Nana was respected in the valley, there was something fearsome about a person on such intimate terms with life and death. Nana knew too much.

Elissa believed that if anyone knew who her parents were, it was surely Nana. After all, it had been Nana who had midwifed Elissa. Nana had guided all of the valley's children into the world, and their parents too. She was as much a natural feature of High Crossing as the river and the mountains, escorting its inhabitants into life, and out of it when their time came, gentling their passage with potions to take away pain and fear. Elissa assumed that it must have been Nana who escorted her mother out, leaving the baby behind, for no valley mother would purposely leave her child to be raised by a stranger.

Elissa gently teased a stalk of timothy grass from its sheath and placed the sweet tip in her mouth. *Nana must know my mother's name,* she thought. But if Nana knew, she was not about to tell Elissa. The only answer she would give to Elissa's queries was "She's dead." Nor had she ever said a word about Elissa's father—to anyone. If she had, Elissa would have been the first one to know, for she had exceedingly sharp ears.

Elissa had always suspected that her father was still alive—not that Nana had dropped so much as a hint in that direction. If anything, she was even more tight-lipped about him than she was about Elissa's mother, which was precisely why Elissa believed he was alive. If he was dead, why not just say so? Nana certainly had no qualms about telling Elissa that her mother was dead. There could be only two explanations. Either he was alive and Nana simply didn't know who or where he was—or Elissa's birth was shameful. That ruled out the valley farmers. Legitimate or not, relatives would have taken her in. But if she were an illegitimate child fathered by someone of birth, that would certainly be a good reason for Nana to keep quiet.

Elissa spit out the blade of grass she had been chewing on. The only problem was that there was no one of nobility besides Lord Bruno at the Manor. Both of Bruno's brothers had died in childhood, and his father had passed away some years before she was born. It was a foolish idea, yet whenever the word "father" crept into her mind, it was Bruno's big brown beard she imagined, his jolly laugh booming through the Manor, his giggling children bouncing on his knee. He was certainly the ideal father.

Elissa propped herself up on her elbows, imagining that her father was out there, somewhere, perhaps looking for her. She gazed at the horizon, letting her mind float down familiar streams, casting her thoughts toward that distant pale rim as a fisherman casts a line.

My father is a trader. He met my beautiful mother at the summer fair and fell instantly and deeply in love with her. Then he went off on an expedition. He meant to return soon but couldn't. . . . His ships were lost at sea, or perhaps he was set upon by robbers in the forest. He didn't want to return empty-handed, so he stayed abroad to build up his fortune until he could come for us. And then something happened. . . .

Elissa's mind swirled into a dark eddy.

Perhaps my father is in prison. . . .

These were treacherous waters.

But he has been imprisoned wrongly for a crime he did not commit. He is languishing right at this very moment in some horrible dungeon. Somehow I will find him and free him from his bondage. He will be proud and grateful, and he will reach out his arms and call me his precious jewel, his brave girl. . . .

Elissa sighed. "Someday I will find him," she solemnly vowed. "I will go to the ends of the earth if I have to, but I will find him."

Now that she had said it aloud, the idea held a certain appeal. She would journey far—to the famed market of Alhamazar, where all traders completed their journeys, and to the eastern shores of Castlemar, where scholars had inscribed all of human knowledge into countless books. They would tell her where to find him. She would sail the Great Sea and climb the circle of mountains that held up the sky.

And when I find him—

Elissa didn't notice the flash of metal on the opposite mountainside, something that caught the edge of the afternoon sun and threw it back like a beacon. Nor did she register the line of animals descending through the eastern pass, even though she was staring straight at it. It was Gertrude's braying—loud and insistent—that brought her mind back to the present. Only then did she spot the men and horses.

A trading party, she thought. *And a large one!*

Jerking herself back to reality, Elissa snatched up her saddlebags and scurried down the side of the mountain, skidding wildly down the grassy slope in her haste. It took nowhere near as long to descend the mountain as it had taken to climb up it. The path to Gertrude's small meadow, while steep, was thankfully short. As she rushed to throw the bags over Gertrude's back, Elissa could barely contain her excitement.

"Silk traders!" she cried. "From the East!"

The donkey swished her tail irritably.

"Sure took you long enough," said Gertrude. "I've been calling you for over an hour."

∽ 2 ∽

The Mysterious Guest

Gertrude stopped abruptly at the Manor wall.

"I'm not carrying you another step," she said. "My hooves are killing me."

"Oh, Gertrude," whispered Elissa.

"Get off," said Gertrude.

Elissa pursed her mouth, but she didn't dare argue with Gertrude this close to the Manor. Nana had warned her enough about keeping her Gift to herself.

Elissa swung down to the ground and slung the saddlebags over her shoulder. With a swish of her tail the donkey ambled off toward the river pasture, where the grass was moist and thick. It was a short walk to Nana's cottage, which lay just past the Manor gardens on a knoll overlooking the river, but Elissa would have preferred riding.

She wanted to finish her chores as quickly as possible in case the traders set up a market.

Walking beside the stone wall, Elissa imagined what kinds of goods the merchants might have brought with them. Surely silks. All caravans from the East brought silks, though very few people in the valley could afford them. Most valley dwellers wove their own cloth from wool they carded and spun themselves, or from linen, which they dyed using local plants. The bright colors and soft texture of Eastern silks brought sighs to the lips of valley maidens, as did the glittering bracelets and earrings that accompanied the cloth, for silk merchants often traded in jewelry as well. Sometimes they also brought ironware, inlaid boxes, and steel pots. If the traders had brought enough goods, Bruno would declare a fair day, in which case there would be a feast with jugglers, pipes, and dancing. Best of all, there would be pies.

If I finish all my chores, thought Elissa, *Nana might give me a copper for the fair.*

She quickened her steps, only to pause at the Manor gate. It was ajar, which was not unusual during the day. What drew her attention was the

19

commotion. Curious, Elissa peered through the gate into the stone courtyard. Inside, dozens of people were bustling about, pushing straw-laden carts, carrying barrels and sacks, leading pigs and geese, and carrying chickens in crates. They were moving in a steady stream toward the Manor. Elissa stepped through the gate and walked across the cobbled courtyard.

The Manor was bursting with activity. Harried-looking housekeepers were sweeping the gray stone floor. Footboys followed behind them, scattering handfuls of soft pine needles as they went and dodging porters who carried sacks and barrels on their shoulders. Some of the more agile household staff had been lifted up to the ceiling, where they were hanging fragrant garlands of white lilies over the thick rafters. Lady Hilde, her plump cheeks flushed, stood in the center of the room organizing their efforts with waving hands and calling instructions to the maids who wove in and out among the young boys and porters, their arms laden with clean bedding, soaps, towels, scrubbing stones, and scents. Elissa looked around the room, seeking out the friendly face of Bruno's hound, Cassius, who normally wandered everywhere, but he was nowhere to be seen.

"Make way!"

Two men jostled past Elissa with loads of firewood. She followed behind them on their way to the kitchen. Nana would very likely be found there, advising Cook on which herbs would place the diners in the most pleasant after-supper mood. Perhaps she would tell Elissa what was going on.

Nana was not in the kitchen. What was more, the room was in a state of chaos. Piles of greens, fruits, and winter tubers were heaped on every table. Spices and dried herbs had been organized and laid out over sheets of white muslin, ready to grind. Bowls of nuts stood ready to crack. The marble pastry slabs were covered with flour, and every pot in the hearth was bubbling. From the quantity and variety of ingredients spread over every surface, it was clear that Cook was intent on surpassing herself, preparing a feast of delicacies the likes of which this household hadn't seen since Bruno's firstborn had come of age. Cook, whose face was flushed as red as the beets she had been chopping, was busy yelling out instructions to her miserable helper. Cook's tantrums, along with her culinary talents, were mighty.

"Mincemeat!" Cook hollered. "And don't you tell me you can't find it, or I'll make some out of you!" Cook lifted the crimson-stained cleaver and waved it at her hapless apprentice, a skinny child of eight or nine with wide, frightened eyes. The girl ducked her head and quickly scuttled out of reach.

Elissa caught the child's arm.

"What's all this about?" she asked.

"Visitors from Castlemar. We got word about two hours ago, and it's been madness ever since," whispered the girl, pulling her arm back. "Now let me go or I'll end up in one of Cook's pies."

Elissa released the frantic apprentice, who instantly scurried off to the larder in search of mincemeat. Catching the baleful look in Cook's eye, Elissa started to back cautiously out of the door, only to feel a heavy hand cover her shoulder. She turned and looked up into Lord Bruno's great brown beard. His woolen tunic was covered with sawdust, and he smelled of horses. Bruno's eyes, normally sparkling with good humor, were serious.

"Elissa," he said with uncharacteristic gravity, "you will dine with our guest in the Great Hall this evening."

He called across the kitchen, telling one of the burly porters to follow him into the cellars, and was gone before Elissa had a chance to utter a reply.

Elissa stood in the doorway dumbfounded, her mouth hanging open. "Step aside!" A man carrying a sack of flour over one shoulder elbowed her out of his path. Elissa left the kitchen perplexed.

Normally feast days were announced publicly. It was very unusual for Bruno to go around making individual invitations. Somebody important must have arrived. *Who is this guest?* she wondered. A silk trader from the East wouldn't be prominent enough to warrant turning out the Great Hall. Usually merchants dined in their own quarters or in the kitchen with the rest of the staff. It was not uncommon for Lord Bruno and even Lady Hilde to join them by the kitchen hearth, as they all loved to hear the news travelers brought. Perhaps it was a delegation of explorers on their way to the Northern Waste, since that region was largely uncharted and populated only by nomadic tribes who, on shaggy horses, followed herds of elk. But explorers didn't seem important enough, either. They were a scruffy lot, and not well behaved. Besides, Bruno had said "guest." Guests were usually people of birth or who held some status. Perhaps that was why Bruno had been so gruff. He hated formality.

Lost in thought, Elissa walked along the path that ran through the kitchen gardens and out into the orchards. She had never been asked to dine with guests before. As a rule, only Bruno's family was allowed such intimate contact with people of status. Elissa had a flash of intuition. Nana was getting old. The last few months she had spent more and more time by the fire, poking at the embers with a distant look on her face. Perhaps Bruno had sent for another healer. If that were the case, it would make perfect sense to invite Elissa. Nana was greatly respected, and her apprentice would have some value to a new healer.

Well, thought Elissa, *Nana would surely know if a new healer was coming. The question is whether she will be willing to tell me anything about it. It would be just like Nana not to say a word.*

The saddlebags were beginning to chafe against her shoulder. Fortunately, she didn't have far to carry them, as Nana's cottage was just a stone's throw from the orchard. Bruno liked to keep Nana close at hand for emergencies.

As Nana's drooping thatched roof appeared through the trees, Elissa's resolve strengthened. Nana would simply *have* to talk to her.

The red and white climbing roses that twined themselves about the stone doorway trembled slightly as Elissa passed beneath them. She entered the cottage, a question on her lips, only to fall silent as soon as she crossed the threshold.

Nana sat on the stool beside her hearth, her head bent forward. If Elissa hadn't known better, she would have said that Nana was reading, but as far as Elissa knew, Nana had never learned to decipher script. She sat completely motionless, hunched over something in her lap. Receiving no acknowledgment, Elissa advanced quietly and stood by the hearth, patiently waiting.

As Elissa stood watching, she suddenly realized how frail Nana looked. Whatever it was she held in her lap could not be seen, but her arms, bare almost to the elbows, looked as fragile as twigs. Elissa felt a slight tremor in her heart. Though Nana was not as affectionate as a true mother, she was the only parent Elissa had ever known.

"Nana," Elissa whispered.

The old woman slowly turned. Her hair was white and her frame shriveled, but her eyes were as bright as ever.

"Did you find the meadowsweet?" she asked. Elissa nodded. "Well, don't dawdle—fetch it here." As Elissa turned to pick up the bags she'd left by the doorway, she thought she caught a glimpse of something white fluttering up from Nana's hands. Then Nana was beside her, rummaging through her saddlebags and muttering under her breath. Elissa cast a glance toward the stool where Nana had been sitting. Nothing was there. Whatever Nana had been examining was gone.

"Nana—" she began.

"Not now. Go hang the meadowsweet before it loses its strength."

There was no use arguing. Like Gertrude, Nana could not be pushed or prodded. As Elissa made her way to the drying shed, she could not help but wish her mother had left her with a woman who *spoke*.

Taking care not to dislodge the delicate blossoms, Elissa removed the flowers from the bags and hung them upside down by their long stalks. Her hands performed the familiar tasks automatically, for her mind was elsewhere. A thought had occurred to her. Nana was as tight as a mussel when it came to releasing useful information, but Gertrude was a terrible gossip. After she finished hanging the flowers, making sure they were not touching any of the other herbs, Elissa slipped away to find Gertrude.

Not every young girl talks to animals. But Elissa, having no one else to talk to as a small child, had simply started to address the creatures around her. One day when she was in her fifth year, and old enough to pasture the animals by herself, she politely remarked that it was a fine afternoon—as she had seen grown-ups do.

"Are you *talking*?" the incredulous donkey had said.

"Yes," Elissa replied, delighted. "I am."

"Humans don't talk," said the donkey.

"I do!" Elissa was quite proud of herself.

27

"Good," said the donkey. "In that case, you can fetch me some oats." Elissa ran off to do as she was bid.

"Gertrude says she wants some oats," she said to Nana.

Nana had looked cross at the interruption. She had been making an infusion that must not be allowed to boil.

"Donkeys don't talk," said Nana absently. "And don't you talk to them either, or people will think you are mad, like Old Woman Paisey."

But Elissa had found a new friend and would not be deterred. "The farmers talk to their animals all the time. They say 'Whoa' and 'Giddyup' and 'Stay.'"

"But the animals don't talk back, do they?"

"No," admitted Elissa. "Not much. They complain when they are tired. But the farmers don't listen."

Nana stopped stirring. "You mean you *understand* them?" asked Nana quietly.

Elissa nodded.

"Do they *all* talk to you?" Nana fixed her eyes on Elissa.

"No," admitted Elissa. "They talk to each other

mostly, and the bugs don't talk at all. The animals won't talk to me unless I talk to them first. That's because they think *we* just make noises."

Nana observed Elissa for a moment with an intensity that Elissa found frightening. It looked like Nana was going to scold her some more. Elissa hung her head in shame. She knew that children were not supposed to start conversations. She'd been very rude. Perhaps she should apologize. Then Nana did a most unexpected and wonderful thing. She reached out and hugged Elissa.

"You have a Gift," said Nana finally.

Perplexed, Elissa had looked around the room but didn't see a gift. She would have liked a doll.

"Can Gertrude have some oats, then?" she asked, emboldened by the rare gesture of affection.

"Of course," said Nana. "But you must *never* tell *anyone* you can talk to animals. Promise."

Elissa had kept her promise and stayed out of earshot of people who might think her crazy—or worse, as Nana explained. There had not been a witch in High Crossing in many years, but people still feared them. In any event it was an

29

easy promise to keep, as people seldom wandered about the cottage grounds.

Whether there were people about or not, Elissa desperately needed to talk to Gertrude. It was nearly time for dinner, and she still had no idea who the mysterious guest might be. Elissa ran lightly down the beaten path that led to the pasture, hoping the donkey would be alone. Sometimes there were other animals pasturing by the riverbank, with young children nearby to watch them. She was relieved to find Gertrude grazing with only a few unattended horses for company.

"Gertrude," she said, "I need to talk to you."

"I'm not carrying you anywhere," said Gertrude. "My back hoof is a mess. And it's all your fault. All that rushing."

"It's not that," she said. "Gertrude, listen, have you heard anything?"

"I hear lots of things," said Gertrude agreeably, her mouth full. "Those silly hens never shut up. All day long it's 'grubs, eggs, grubs, eggs.' I could die of boredom."

"No, *no.* I mean the caravan. The one that just arrived. Have their horses said anything at all?"

"Well...," began Gertrude slowly. "I've heard that the journey was long and hard, and they'd give anything for a couple of weeks in pasture, which, I might add, they are not likely to get."

"Why not?" breathed Elissa.

Gertrude chewed and swallowed. "There is not a single mule among them, so they are not traders. And..." Gertrude paused. "The men are all carrying swords, so they won't be staying long."

"What do you mean?" asked Elissa, not comprehending.

Gertrude turned her head until she was looking full into Elissa's face.

"They're soldiers," she said. "And they're armed for battle."

Nana was not in her customary place beside the hearth when Elissa returned. Nor was she to be found in the drying shed. It was just as well. Elissa needed to be alone. There was so much to think about, her head felt close to bursting. Why had soldiers come to the valley? Who was the guest? And why did Bruno want her to meet him? All the unanswered questions had started to rattle around in her head like seeds in a dry gourd. She needed to give her head a rest. And what was even more important, she needed to change her clothes. Gathering her skirts in one hand, she climbed up the narrow ladder that led from the storeroom to the attic.

The rays of the late afternoon sun were already slanting through the two south dormers, tinting the alcoves beneath them with gold. She walked to the closer of the two alcoves, in which there was a straw mattress. This was where Elissa had slept since she was a small child, and along with a small box of toiletries and a few clothes, it constituted the entirety of her "private chambers." The other alcove held a locked trunk. Elissa removed her clothing down to her shift, letting her skirt and blouse fall to the floor. She intended to change into her clean shirt and tunic, but instead she found herself squatting in front of the trunk.

The trunk was a mystery. It had rested in its alcove for as long as Elissa had slept in hers. She had never seen Nana move it or open it. Elissa traced the delicate carving on the front of the

32

trunk with her forefinger. It was clearly not made in the valley. Farmers valued strength and function over rich ornamentation. The twining vines and flowers that covered the top and sides of the box served no purpose other than to delight the eyes, and for years Elissa had taken pleasure in them. It was hard to imagine such a thing belonging to Nana—not only because it was beautiful, but because it was locked. Nana had no need for a locked box. She had no gold or silver to guard, no precious jewels.

Elissa reached under the eaves for the little pick she kept hidden behind a rafter. After years of practice picking the lock, she had no need of a key.

Once released, the lid opened easily. Without hesitation, Elissa put her hands inside, confidently turning back the folds of cloth that lay within. The trunk's contents were as familiar to her as the mattress she slept on. Inside was a silk dress of lustrous forest green with matching slippers and an embroidered sash. There was also a woven hairnet laced with tiny glistening pearls, and a bone hair ornament of the kind worn by the Northern tribes. These could hardly have been Nana's garments. The old healer of the valley had obviously never been young. Besides, Elissa could not imagine Nana in such bright colors. She was as drab as a bowerbird. Elissa lifted the silk dress from its plain white cotton wrapper. Its soft folds slithered over her fingers— so light they seemed to be made of air.

As she held it up, the cloth caught the light and gave it back—a sign of fine silk and fine dye. Anyone could tell that the cloth for this dress had been woven in the East, and that it had been costly. Elissa could not imagine how Nana could have come by such a dress. A gown like this was meant for royalty. And there was no royalty in High Crossing. Lady Hilde, while the mistress of the Manor, was a down-to-earth, unpolished soul, well suited to the rough-and-tumble ways of her husband and to the rigors of managing a large farm estate. She was also quite buxom. The dress certainly did not belong to Hilde. When she was younger, Elissa had liked to imagine that the dress had once belonged to her mother. Simply caressing the soft fabric had eased her loneliness and blunted the ache of abandonment.

Whoever owned this dress was slim and elegant—and at least two inches taller than Elissa. The last time she'd tried it on; it had fallen off her shoulders.

Elissa lifted the dress experimentally against her chest. A small white moth fluttered out, delicately brushing against her cheek before disappearing. Elissa ignored the insect, as it was not the kind that laid its eggs in cloth. Then, on a sudden impulse, she slipped out of her shift and into the luminous gown.

Elissa was enormously pleased to discover that it fit—as did the slippers. The gown's fitted bodice made her stand a little straighter, and when she stood tall, the hem just brushed the floor. Elissa stood there for a moment, pensively swishing the dress around her as an idea formed in her mind.

She looked at her humble pile of clothing, the homespun skirt faded with washing and the white linen blouse. Both garments had seen their fair share of hard use, as had her dull brown tunic. No matter who this guest was—trader, healer, or soldier—she should look her finest for her first dinner in the Great Hall. And what could be finer than this dress? Lord Bruno would be proud of her. And Nana . . .

Nana will strangle me, thought Elissa. Even if it wasn't Nana's dress, it certainly wasn't Elissa's, and in the valley there was no crime more shameful than theft. She would be disgraced if the true owner found out. Elissa hesitated for a moment. She would just have to make sure that Nana didn't see her. Later, when Nana found out—if she found out—the dress would already have been put back safely in its trunk with no harm done. And if Nana was still angry . . . Elissa decided that she would ford that river when she came to it. Tonight, making a good appearance was more important than Nana's ire.

Elissa wound the sash around her waist, letting it fall in two equal lengths down the front of the skirt. She adjusted it so the embroidery showed to its full advantage. She picked up the bone ornament, considered it, but chose the net instead. Her hair was much too thick for ornaments. She twisted her hair up into a roll and stretched the net into place, checking it to make sure no stray locks had escaped.

Oh, for a mirror, she thought. She descended the ladder carefully, lifting her dress to her knees with one hand to prevent the flowing skirts from picking up bits of straw. From the silence in the cottage, Elissa knew Nana was not downstairs. That was strange, but convenient. Normally Nana would be banging around among her pots at this hour, calling for Elissa to find this or that for her. Elissa took Nana's absence as a Sign—she was meant to wear the dress.

Elissa worked her way around the hearth, avoiding a pile of charcoal, baskets of dried herbs, and scattered soot-stained pots. A small movement from among the pots startled her. It was Willie, the cat, hunting for his evening meal.

"Oh!" said Elissa. "It's you. Have you seen Nana?"

The cat sat down and licked his back. "No," he said. "Have you seen any mice?"

"No," said Elissa, not that she would tell Willie if she had. As far as hunting was concerned, animals were on their own. She took a few steps toward the door and turned. "How do I look, Willie?"

The cat turned his luminous eyes to her. "Like a human."

Typical cat, thought Elissa, stepping cautiously through the doorway.

The sun had set and the twilight hour had begun. Soon supper would be served. Elissa hurried to the Manor, flitting through the darkening orchard like a bat. She had forgotten to carry a lamp, but she knew the path so well, she could travel it blindfolded. By the time Elissa arrived at the Manor gate, she was completely out of breath. She crossed the courtyard confident that Nana hadn't seen her. At the double oak doors she hesitated for a moment and patted her hair. Then she pushed the doors open. The main hall was empty. Sounds of merriment drifted from the kitchen wing. She turned and made her way to the arch that led to the Great Hall. Elissa's heart was beating a dance rhythm in her chest, but she was sure she had made the right decision. She took a deep breath and crossed the threshold.

To her surprise, there was only one table, at the far end of the Hall. She had expected several, at least enough to accommodate all the travelers, if not all of Lord Bruno's children and friends. The single table looked somehow more imposing, not less, for occupying a room that could have held a hundred people. A candelabra had been lit at the center of the table, but the rest of the room was dim. Elissa peered across the room, trying to identify the people at the table. Lord Bruno occupied the center, his broad shoulders looking cramped in his formal doublet. Lady Hilde sat to his right, her face gleaming in the candlelight. Beside her a man, his face hidden in shadows, was whispering in her ear. Lady Hilde was leaning slightly back, away from him, her face averted. To Bruno's left sat another unfamiliar man, dressed in a close-fitting black doublet. Elissa stood immobile in the doorway, waiting for Bruno to notice her. She had no idea what to do. Should she enter or wait? Fortunately, Bruno beckoned and stood, or she might have waited forever.

As she stepped inside, the man at Bruno's left rose as well. Though most of his body was obscured by shadow, she could see that he was a lean man. She could tell from the straight line of his shoulders and the confident angle of his chin that he was used to wielding authority. His narrow face was dominated by a haughty, high-bridged nose, and his eyes, regarding her intently beneath drawn brows, were sharp. Unlike most valley men, he wore no beard, which made his expression easy to read. At the moment he looked like a hawk that had just spotted a hare.

There was silence in the Hall until Bruno spoke. He said only one word: "Elissa." She didn't know if she should curtsy, or, indeed, if it mattered what she did, for Bruno was no longer looking at her but at the man who stood to his left. The man nodded. Bruno turned toward Elissa, gesturing to the man beside him.

"Lord Falk, High Lord of the Eastern Reach, firstborn to the throne of Castlemar."

Bruno stated Lord Falk's titles slowly, deliberately. Then he paused as though waiting for a sign of recognition on Elissa's part. There was none, as these titles were entirely meaningless to her.

"Come, Elissa. Meet your father."

❧ 3 ❧

A Long Journey

Bruno has made a mistake, thought Elissa.

The man facing her from across the room was someone whom she would never in her wildest dreams have imagined as her father. For one thing, he was a noble! Moreover, with his black hair and dark eyes, he didn't resemble her in the least. How on earth could this man be her father?

"Come." Bruno beckoned again. Elissa took a few hesitant steps, then made her way across the room. She couldn't take her eyes off Lord Falk, who regarded her fixedly from under his dark brows. *This can't possibly be true,* she thought. But she didn't say a word, nor did she curtsy when she reached the table. The dark man did not smile when Bruno invited her to sit next to him. He

41

gave her only one sharp glance and then turned to Bruno, continuing their conversation.

All during the meal Elissa held very still, trying to blend in with the chair, the table, the floor. She didn't know what she would say if he spoke to her. *Don't notice me,* she prayed.

And indeed, he didn't. Lord Falk conversed with Bruno in a manner that managed to be both terse and fluid, sociable yet unrevealing. She listened, but understood little. There was talk about the drought in Castlemar and about various lords whose names she did not recognize. Lord Falk asked her one question, and one question only.

"Can you ride?"

Elissa only nodded. Lord Falk gave her the strong impression that the less she said, the better. Besides, if she said anything at all, she was bound to make a fool of herself. She risked a brief sidelong glance at his face. He was looking not at her but down the table, at the shadowy man Bruno had introduced as Kreel. It was an odd name, matching an unpleasant face.

"Good," said Lord Falk. "We will be leaving tomorrow."

Leaving? Elissa lost her ability to focus.

Cook's meal, in truth the rival of any ever served in the Great Hall, went unnoticed. Lord Falk ate his food but seemed unimpressed by the pies, puddings, and confections Cook had spent the afternoon preparing. Leaving aside the meat dishes, Elissa put forkfuls of honeyed beets, parsnip fritters, and fig pie in her mouth. She couldn't taste a thing, which was a pity. Cook's pies were legendary.

After they had dined, Lord Falk rose. It was clear the meal was at an end. Elissa sensed that she was being dismissed, so she rose as well. She may or may not have said "Good night" when he bade her a good evening. Then she crossed the floor just as she had entered, only on slightly shakier legs. She felt Lord Falk watching her as she left the room.

Indeed, Falk was watching her, though not even Elissa could have read his expression. Falk's was a face that could be opened or closed at will. Once Elissa was gone, he thanked Bruno and Hilde for their hospitality and retired to his rooms. His longtime Captain of the Guard, Aldric, was waiting for him, stationed outside his door as if he were standing watch. Aldric's craggy face was grave as he greeted his lord.

"Aldric," said Falk, "I trust you and the men have eaten."

"Yes, my lord," said Aldric, inclining his head. "Quite well."

"And will the horses be ready by tomorrow?" asked Falk.

"I have attended to everything, my lord," said Aldric.

"You always do," said Falk, entering the room. He gestured for Aldric to follow and watched as Aldric closed the door.

"Is it confirmed, then?" asked Aldric. "Is the girl really your daughter?"

Falk was silent for a moment.

"There is no doubt in my mind," Falk said finally.

"Ah," said Aldric. "Then the plans will go ahead."

"They will," said Falk, sitting to remove his boots.

Aldric remained standing. "And what if she does not wish to come with us?" asked Aldric.

"She will do as she is told," said Falk curtly. He fell silent again.

"What is it?" Aldric was adept at reading his lord's silences.

Falk hesitated before speaking. "She is very quiet," he said.

Aldric nodded. "Do you think she understands what is expected of her?"

"No," said Falk. "She has no idea. Kreel was listening to every word I said. There was no opportunity to speak. Even so, she hardly said a word."

"Is she—" Aldric didn't know how to put it. "Slow?"

Falk rose to his feet, took Aldric by the arm, and led him to the door. "Perhaps. But that may be for the best. The less inquisitive she is, the better she will serve our purpose."

Elissa walked back to the cottage on feet that felt nothing. She was not sure of what had just transpired in the Great Hall, or who that dark man really was, but one thing she knew for certain was that he was not her father. Up ahead the trees parted, revealing the roof of Nana's cottage, frosted lightly by moonlight. As she put her hand on the door, she felt a soft body rub against her leg.

"The Old Woman is back," said Willie.

Elissa reached down and stroked the cat absently. "Thanks," she said, thinking it really didn't matter anymore if Nana felt cross about the dress. She opened the door and walked in. Nana was in her place by the hearth, looking as if she hadn't moved all day.

"I see you found the dress," said Nana.

Elissa hung her head, embarrassed.

"Just put it back where you found it." Surprisingly, Nana didn't look angry.

"Lord Bruno invited me to dinner—" Elissa began in her own defense.

"Yes, child," said Nana impatiently. "I know." Nana waved to Elissa. "Come sit down. It's hurting my neck to look up at you."

Elissa picked up a stool and placed it before Nana. There were so many questions in her mind, so much confusion; all she wanted was to put her head in Nana's lap. And if she had ever done so before, she might have. Her head hurt terribly.

46

"There was a man, Nana," she said. "Lord Bruno said he was my father."

"Ah," said Nana, poking at the fire. "Then he is."

"He can't be, Nana," cried Elissa. "He's a *lord*!"

"That hardly matters," said Nana sharply. "Lords sire children as well as peasants. The question is, who are *you*?"

Elissa looked away. All her life she had been "the orphan." Now that a father had appeared, she didn't know how to think of herself. "I don't know," she said finally.

"If you don't know, then you could be the daughter of a lord." Nana looked directly at Elissa. "You could be anything."

"I suppose," said Elissa wearily. "But I don't believe it."

For the second time in Elissa's memory, Nana did something motherly. She reached out and touched Elissa's hair, looking deeply into her eyes. Set in their nests of wrinkles, Nana's eyes gleamed like shiny black stones. Elissa couldn't see the whites at all. For a moment Elissa had the strangest feeling that she wasn't looking at Nana's eyes, but that she was looking *through* them, into another creature's eyes—something not human.

"Believe it," said Nana.

Elissa fell asleep as soon as her head hit the pillow. She passed the night in a deep, dreamless sleep until the dawn marbled the walls of her alcove. As she opened her eyes to the new day, the memory of the previous night rushed in like a blast of cold air, rousing her completely. She had a real living father! And she was a complete fool.

What on earth was I thinking? she marveled. *How could I have doubted Lord Bruno?* She had acted like a dunce! After being introduced to Lord Falk—her father—all she could do was stand there. She hadn't said a word. How rude he must have thought her. What poor manners she'd shown. She hadn't curtsied or bowed, and what was worse, she had hardly paid attention to anything he'd said. Why, she hadn't even heard where they were going. And they were leaving today! Elissa struck her forehead with the palm of her hand.

"I'm *such* an idiot," she muttered. "And I didn't even tell Nana."

Well, there wasn't much time to prepare, and she had farewells to make. Dear Gertrude. How could she ever tell Gertrude she was leaving? The poor old thing would be crushed. And Nana? With Elissa gone, how would she manage? She'd have to break the news gently. Elissa rose, slipped hurriedly into her blouse and skirt, and scuttled down the ladder. Nana was there by the fire, as always. She passed a steaming bowl of oats to Elissa.

"For fortitude," she said. "You will need to gather your strength for the journey."

Elissa sighed. Apparently Nana already knew she was leaving. Maybe Bruno had told her. Nana passed her a mug of tea.

"What's in this?" asked Elissa, staring into the mug. It had an odor that she couldn't identify.

Nana smiled privately as she stirred one of the many clay pots that simmered in the crackling embers.

"Something to give you patience," she said.

Nana sat on her stool, quietly observing Elissa while she gulped down her breakfast. Elissa was in a frenzy of excitement.

"Nana—" Elissa began.

49

"Be off with you now." The old woman turned away and resumed her stirring. "I have work to do, and there's no time for talk."

Elissa stared at Nana's hunched back. Not for the first time, she wished Nana could be a different person, somebody who would say "Now there, tell me all about it" instead of "Be off with you"—someone who would answer her questions, who would put her mind to rest. Swallowing her frustration, Elissa made her way to the stable.

"You're late," said Gertrude. "I was getting hungry."

Elissa opened the gate and walked beside Gertrude to the low pasture by the river that was Gertrude's favorite breakfast spot.

Elissa picked up a stone and threw it into the river. "Nana never talks to me." Her voice was bitter.

"She never talks to me either," said Gertrude, beginning to munch.

"But she is *supposed* to talk to me," said Elissa. "She just *won't*."

"Well, you can't turn a crow into a canary,"

mumbled Gertrude, a tuft of grass between her teeth.

"I suppose not," Elissa admitted. The pressure in her chest eased. She always felt better when she talked to Gertrude. A thought suddenly occurred to her. *What will I do without Gertrude?*

"Oh, Gertrude," said Elissa, "I have to leave today!"

Gertrude lowered her head to the grass again. "I figured you'd be going somewhere when they got Bessie dressed up last night," she said, munching busily. "Horses have all the fun."

Elissa groaned.

"Bessie got new shoes and everything. They brushed her down and fussed over her like she was going to the races," continued Gertrude. "I *never* get that kind of attention." Gertrude looked pointedly at Elissa while she chewed.

"Gertrude, have they—"

"I wish I had shoes like that. Not that I need them. I *know* where I'm putting my feet. That new saddle blanket is nice, though."

"Gertrude! Pay attention! Has anybody said anything about where we're going?"

Gertrude looked up, chewing thoughtfully. "Not a whinny. You'd think they were on a secret mission. And that black horse over there by the fence is not a local breed. He has a funny way of talking."

Elissa looked over toward the fence and spotted an elegant gelding. As she watched, his delicate head turned on a smoothly arched neck to meet her gaze.

"Desert horse," said Gertrude. "Pretty, but not too bright. You have to watch out for those aristocratic breeds. They can turn nasty. And they lose something after a few generations, if you know what I mean."

Elissa's eyes clouded.

Gertrude took a step backward. "Are your eyes going to leak?"

"No," said Elissa. "It's just that it's not exactly what I expected."

"What isn't?" asked Gertrude, still chewing.

"For one thing, I didn't expect to be leaving you." Elissa fell silent. "And he isn't what I expected either."

"Who?"

"My father," she said. "He's a lord, and that's

wonderful, I suppose, but he hardly said anything to me at all, which isn't his fault, because I didn't say anything to him, either. But still—"

Gertrude snorted. "He sired you. Isn't that enough?"

Elissa chewed on her lip. "No," she said, "it isn't. He's supposed to . . ." Her voice trailed away. Elissa could not identify what she was feeling. It was exhilarating to discover that she finally had a real father, but something was wrong.

"What?" asked Gertrude. "I hate it when you don't finish sentences."

The image of Falk's severe face swam into Elissa's mind. "He's supposed to *like* me," she said. "I don't know how to make that happen." She didn't dare say more. Elissa's fantasies of a daring rescue and loving reunion seemed so childish to her today. Now that the dream of a kind, gentle, affectionate father had been replaced by reality— this hard-faced *noble*—she was at a loss. Soon she would leave her home with this man with no idea of what she was supposed to say, or do, or be.

"You try too hard," said Gertrude.

Elissa was overcome with homesickness. What if she never returned to the valley? What would she do without Gertrude? She flung her arms around the donkey's sturdy neck.

"Oh, Gertrude," she cried, "I am going to miss you so much!"

"Now you *are* leaking," Gertrude grumbled. "You'll be just fine. Bessie is a responsible lass. She'll look after you. And she has the strongest set of teeth in the stable. Not to mention that kick of hers. Now let go before I suffocate." Gertrude's gruff tone did not put Elissa off, nor did it make her let go. She knew Gertrude didn't really mind. Elissa held on another few minutes, until Gertrude nudged her on her way.

Elissa returned home by way of the river, walking slowly. The water curled and eddied past the grassy banks, flowing to unknown lands. Who knew where she would end up? For all she knew, Falk could be taking her to the ends of the earth. She stopped to watch a mother wood duck, out for a swim with her brood.

"Darlings," she called, squatting by the shallows, "will you miss me?"

The ducklings, still covered in gray down, paddled close. They nibbled tenderly at her outstretched fingers.

"You'll always have *us*," said the ducks.

It was true. No matter where she went, there would always be animals to talk to—her secret friends.

"Thank you," she said gratefully. "That's a comfort."

By the time she arrived back at the cottage, it was nearly noon, which meant there would only be a little time to talk to Nana before she left.

She climbed up to the attic, thinking that she might never sleep under its sweet thatched roof again. She opened the box that held her few possessions—a tunic, a linen shift, simple under-clothes, an extra shirt, a comb and a brush, and a sewing kit containing two spools of strong thread and a few precious needles.

She held the brush in her hand. As the daughter of a lord, she imagined he would want her to look neat at all times. She squinted at her feet. She'd probably be expected to wear shoes everywhere—perhaps even indoors. She frowned. Who knew what else her relatives would expect of her? She could only hope that they would be forgiving—after all, they were family.

Elissa packed slowly, putting her basic toiletries

and sewing kit onto a square of linen. She folded her clothing on top: shirt, underclothes, shift, and tunic. Elissa fingered the coarse wool of the tunic and put it back. She'd have no need for such a rustic garment in Castlemar. She glanced with longing at the box containing the silk dress. But it was bad enough that she had stolen it once. Nana would never forgive her for stealing it twice.

There was a squat beeswax candle beside her bed, which she placed on top of the pile. She had no concept of what else she might need. Perhaps some of Nana's remedies might be useful. There could be all manner of injuries on this trip—cuts, bruises, illnesses. Elissa tied the ends of the cloth together and descended the ladder to the storeroom, balancing the bundle on her head. She was picking through a rack of small brown bottles when she heard Nana's muted voice. Elissa hadn't even realized that Nana was home. Hiding behind the open door, she poked her head cautiously around the doorframe, trying to see who had come to visit.

A dark silhouette blocked the front door. Nana rose and repeated her invitation.

"Enter," she said. "And be welcome."

The figure materialized into Lord Falk, clad all in black as he had been the night before. Somehow, coming up the path to Nana's door, he hadn't made a sound.

"Do you fare well this morning, my lord?" asked Nana formally. It was not like her to inquire after a man's well-being unless it was to evaluate which type of tincture, potion, or salve might be most appropriate for whatever ailed him. "Will you take some tea?"

Lord Falk nodded and sat on one of the low wooden stools that Nana kept by the fire. In spite of his surroundings, he looked as if he were seated on a throne. Elissa peered into the smoky room, trying to make out his expression. But his face remained shadowed.

Nana passed him a steaming clay mug and watched him while he drank.

The first sip seemed to relax him, for he released his tight grip on the mug.

"Mistress," he began, "I have come in person to give you my thanks."

Nana nodded graciously.

57

"You have done well by my daughter," said Falk.

"She is healthy and strong—fit for the task that lies ahead." Nana nodded her head slightly as she spoke.

Falk's reference to "my daughter" threw Elissa off. It took her a moment to realize that Lord Falk was talking about *her*. Those words produced a strange feeling in her.

"I am glad for that," said Falk. "You have protected her and kept her safe."

"Yes, I have," said Nana. She held up her hand. "All these years, only these four walls have known her true identity."

Realization swept over Elissa in a wave, nearly choking her. A slow flush of heat spread over her cheeks. She took a step backward, inadvertently brushing against a bundle of dried rushes. Nana cocked a sharp eye toward the back room. Gathering her skirts, Elissa retreated quietly.

Falk rose. "Your service shall be rewarded," he said, placing something in Nana's lap. Then he turned abruptly and left, a shadow dissolving into the light. He did not hear Nana's soft reply.

"I have already been rewarded."

Nana listened to the fire pop and hiss for a moment or two before she addressed the back room. "Are you ready, child?"

Elissa entered the room, gripping her bag in her clenched fist.

"Nana!" Elissa's voice was thick with accusation. "You knew the whole time! You knew where to find him!"

"I had my reasons," Nana said.

"What reasons?" cried Elissa. "What reason could you possibly have had for keeping me hidden from my own father?"

"Hiding you was what kept you alive," said Nana evenly.

Elissa's mouth hung open in utter disbelief. "*How?* I am strong and healthy. You said so yourself! My life wasn't in danger!"

"Yes, it was, child. And thanks to me, you are living." Nana spoke in such a calm, matter-of-fact tone of voice that Elissa's burst of anger, having nothing to stoke it, rapidly dissipated, to be replaced by bewilderment and doubt.

"Come here, girl." Nana crooked a withered finger at Elissa.

Elissa approached reluctantly. Her life had

been dominated by this woman, by her secrets, her silences. But if it was impossible to love Nana, it was equally impossible to hate her. Nana had been the only person in Elissa's life who really mattered. And she was very, very old.

"Why, Nana?" whispered Elissa.

"Soon all your questions will be answered. Once you've gone." There was so much quiet conviction in Nana's voice that Elissa believed her. Elissa's throat tightened.

"Nana," Elissa said, "who will feed the chickens? Who will gather your herbs, and hang them up, and make your food, and fetch firewood? Who will light your fire for you?"

"Don't fret, child. I can take care of all that. You have more important tasks at hand. You have a long journey ahead of you, and much to find on your way." Nana nodded her head again. Her eyes grew distant.

"Will you be here when—" Elissa didn't know how to continue. She hardly knew if she would be coming back at all.

"I will be at your journey's end," said Nana.

Elissa felt on the verge of tears. She bit her lip, hard.

Nana reached into her lap. "Here." She thrust a small velvet purse into Elissa's hand. It jingled slightly. "Go ahead, look inside."

Elissa eased the purse strings open and spilled the three gleaming coins into her palm. "Gold!" she gasped. Falk's payment.

"I have no use for gold," said Nana. "Just take care that thieves don't get it."

Elissa felt shaky at the thought. *Thieves?* Suddenly she felt prey to all kinds of threats.

"And take this as well." Nana handed her a small tin of salve. "It's heal-all." Heal-all did just what its name implied, but only when Nana made it. Nobody else in the valley could duplicate the salve.

Elissa looked around the familiar room one last time—its bare stone walls stained with soot, the pots bubbling in the fire, the smell of smoke and sage and thyme.

"Now be on your way," ordered the old woman. "The world awaits, and time's a-wasting."

Then, without another word, she pushed Elissa out the door, and into the world.

≈ 4 ≈

Five Questions

As Elissa walked through the orchard, Cassius came bounding down the path. She patted him on the head.

"They're looking for you," said Cassius. "The Master keeps turning his head this way and that, the way people do when they are looking for something. And he pointed toward your house several times. It would be so much easier if the other humans could talk the way you do."

"Thanks, Cassius. Maybe they will learn someday." Elissa doubted that would ever happen. People weren't honest enough to talk with animals; they kept secrets. No animal could ever understand them. "I am leaving today."

Cassius trotted alongside her. "That's too bad," said the dog. "You've been good company."

"So have you, Cassius." Elissa stopped and fondled his ears. "I wish you could come. It would be nice to have someone from home with me."

Cassius lapped her hand. "Sorry. I have to stay here and protect the Master. Who knows what kind of trouble he would get into without me. He can't even capture his own meat without help."

They were too close to the gardens for Elissa to reply. With a brief "Goodbye," Cassius bounded off.

Elissa continued walking, skirting the gardens and following the wall until she came to the gate. The horses were assembled in the courtyard, their newly shod hooves striking against the cobbles impatiently. A dozen armed soldiers tended their mounts, tightening saddle straps, adjusting stirrups, and checking harnesses. Elissa wondered at their swords and quivers. The Eastern Reach was not a dangerous place for travelers. Not one of the soldiers looked at her as she passed, which was not surprising. To them she appeared to be just another farmer's daughter. She continued on to the Manor, where, no doubt, the rest of the traveling party was gathered.

Bruno and Lord Falk were talking in the main hall—Falk still dressed entirely in black and looking in command. Bruno had forsaken his formal evening attire for his usual country clothes: a jerkin, leather breeches, and linen shirt. There were two other men standing with them. Elissa recognized one from the dinner—Kreel. He was wrapped in a dark cloak, frowning. The other was a tall, light-haired man with a careworn face, standing immediately behind Kreel, his hand resting lightly on his sword hilt. Bruno was talking with Lord Falk, but he stopped when he saw Elissa.

"There you are!" said Bruno.

Lord Falk looked at her bundle. He raised an eyebrow. "Is that all you are bringing with you? We have a wagon, you know."

Elissa flushed with embarrassment. "It's all I have, my lord," she said.

"Ah," said Kreel, moving closer to her. "That will soon be remedied." Then he smiled.

Kreel's smile was the most unnerving thing Elissa had ever seen. His teeth, emerging from beneath his mustache, had been filed to points.

Elissa could not help but think of a shark. Travelers sometimes sold necklaces of shark teeth at market, accompanying their sales patter with horrific stories. She backed away.

"'My lord' will not be necessary," said Lord Falk. "You may call me Falk." He looked down at her with cold eyes. "Or Father."

Elissa nodded, but she was not sure she could comply. Not only was he the most lordly of men, he was also the most unfatherly.

"Yes, my lord," she said.

Lord Falk did not smile.

A soldier entered and announced that the wagons and horses were ready. In a twinkling they were out the door and into the courtyard. Before she mounted her horse—it was not Bessie, to her dismay—Bruno reached down and wrapped his huge arms around her. Then he lifted her onto her horse.

"Safe journey," he said.

Elissa blinked rapidly and swallowed. The order was given, and before she knew it Bruno, and Cassius, and Gertrude, and Willie, and Nana, and the Manor were gone.

Falk's party proceeded directly to the south. Elissa was perplexed. She had assumed that Falk was planning to take her east, to his holdings in Castlemar. But instead of crossing over the eastern pass the way it had come, the caravan followed the river south and then cut west into the wilderness, a huge expanse of forest. The wilderness, as far as Elissa knew, was not on the way to anywhere.

As the forest loomed before her, Elissa could not help but recall the tales travelers told of cutthroats, thieves, and bandits, and ravenous beasts that ate unwary travelers who had been robbed and left defenseless. Nobody from the valley was foolish enough to venture into these strange, dark woods. Elissa was not afraid of beasts, ravenous or otherwise, but as they abandoned the cheerful open meadows of the valley, and the branches closed overhead, her neck hairs rose and her back crawled, as if something were following her. She tried to fill her mind with thoughts of home. She remembered the warmth of Bruno's embrace and tried to retain it. But as the miles gathered under her horse's hooves, the memory faded and grew cold.

Falk's soldiers kept up a good pace. The road was narrow, so they rode two abreast, with Lord Falk heading up the line. Beside him rode the man they called Kreel, on that haughty black horse of his. Kreel frightened her, even though he smiled often—or, more likely, *because* he smiled often. It was just as well he rode at a distance from her. Elissa was accompanied by the Captain of the Guard, Aldric. The captain reminded her of an old tree—tall, straight, and enduring. And his craggy face might have been made of wood, for all the emotion it showed. There were four soldiers ahead of her. They appeared young but capable. The swords hanging at their sides looked like they had been used. Eight more soldiers rode behind. Of Lord Falk she saw little, and heard even less. Twice he rode back along the line. On these occasions Falk hardly acknowledged her presence. For the most part they rode in silence, accompanied only by the clanking of harnesses. Even the horses preferred to keep to themselves, but in any case Elissa could hardly start a conversation with so many people around. At the end of the day she knew no more about their purpose or destination than she had when they started.

On the first night of the journey they made camp in a small clearing. Elissa, tired and sore from riding, retreated to her tent while supper was being prepared, but try as she might, she could not rest. There was too much to think about. Where were they going? She wished she could speak with Lord Falk for just a few moments. There were so many questions she wanted to ask. Did he have other children in Castlemar? She could have grandparents, aunts, uncles, cousins—a whole family. Elissa wondered how they would take to her. Most of all, she wanted to ask about her mother—her looks, her manner, her likes, her dislikes. Falk held all the keys to her past. But that awful Kreel stuck to his side like a leech. Who was he? Nana's cautions about thieves came to mind. Kreel looked like the sort of person who would have no qualms about stealing three gold coins from a young girl.

Elissa rose and lit her candle. Someone, no doubt under orders from Lord Falk, had exchanged her humble square of linen for a sturdy pack. The small kit in which she kept her sewing supplies lay in the bottom. She tossed her shift, her undergarments, and her extra blouse on the cot. She fished a needle and thread out of the kit, and with her teeth she ripped open a corner in the hem of her cloak. One by one she sewed the three gold coins into the hem, separating them with several stitches so they would not clank together.

She lifted the cloak up against her face, feeling the rough texture of homespun cloth. It still smelled of the valley, of meadows and chamomile and sunlight. A single coarse gray hair poked out from between the threads—Gertrude's. Her eyes misted.

A sudden shriek stopped her tears. Elissa threw her cloak over her shoulders and peeked through the tent flap. Two guards sat flanking the entrance. "What's the matter?" she asked. "Who is hurt?"

The guard on the left shrugged.

The shrieking had intensified. Both guards turned and looked toward the trees. Within a moment or two Kreel ran into the clearing, his clothing in disarray, clutching at his posterior with one hand and waving frantically at his head with the other. He was howling at the top of his lungs.

"What's wrong with him?" Elissa wondered why the guards didn't seem concerned. The howls were awful.

"He . . . uh . . . was responding to the call of Nature, Miss," said the guard on the right. He scratched his blond head with the hilt of his sword. "It looks like he got too close to a hornet's nest."

"Way too close," said the other guard. He was trying not to laugh, and not succeeding very well.

Kreel disappeared inside his tent, and soon Elissa spied Aldric making his way across the clearing.

"Aldric will pull out the stingers. He'll do a real *careful* job," said the blond guard. The other guard snorted.

Soon a small group of soldiers gathered around Kreel's tent. Judging from the heckling of the soldiers, it appeared that Kreel was not well liked.

Elissa wondered if she should volunteer her

services as a nurse. The man was repulsive, but she had Nana's salve, and wasn't it her duty to care for the injured? She ducked back inside her tent and found the tin among her belongings. By the time she opened the tent flap again, her two guards were gone. *They are probably with the others,* thought Elissa, *enjoying the evening's entertainment.* Elissa headed purposefully toward Kreel's tent, but before she could offer her assistance, she was waylaid by Lord Falk.

"Come with me," murmured Falk in a low voice as he took her by the arm. He led her to the side of camp that was farthest from Kreel's tent and invited her to sit on a fallen log with him.

"I have to say," said Lord Falk, "those hornets couldn't have picked a better person—or place."

Elissa couldn't suppress a giggle, at which Lord Falk's features creased into something resembling a smile, faint but recognizable. For a moment he looked boyish, almost accessible. Was this the face her mother had loved? Then the smile vanished, and Falk's features resumed their habitual stern arrangement. Elissa dropped her eyes, disappointed, but also hopeful. Perhaps, if she said and did the right things, the smile would return.

Falk spoke without preamble. "You must resent me for the way I have disrupted your life."

Elissa looked up at Falk, flustered. He sounded almost apologetic. She would not have taken Falk as the sort of man to offer an apology. And, in fact, he spoke so stiffly it didn't sound like one. Nevertheless, she was grateful and tried to voice the sentiments of a proper daughter. "You are my father. How could I resent you?" she said.

"How indeed," murmured Falk, so softly that Elissa was not sure she had heard him correctly. His outward expression did not change. But she suddenly realized that he was gazing directly at her. There was something in his eyes that she could not quite identify.

"Your mother's dress suited you," he said.

It took a moment for Elissa to realize what Falk was referring to. "You mean that dress belonged to my mother?"

"Yes," said Falk. "I had it made for her." He paused, as if a thought had just occurred to him. "Has the healer told you nothing?"

Elissa shook her head. "Other than to say she had died, Nana never spoke to me about my mother," she answered.

Falk looked as if he didn't believe her.

"Nana doesn't explain things," she said. "Nana is different from other people." Elissa grew silent. Nana was *very* different. No mother would have sent her daughter away with strangers. But then, Nana wasn't her mother, and this dark stranger *was* her father.

Falk fell silent as well. His brow was furrowed, as if he wanted to say something to her but could not find the words. Elissa looked at his narrow, aristocratic lips pursed in thought, his high brow. All the words she needed to hear were contained in his head. She took a chance.

"Shall we play a game?" she ventured.

Falk's face turned to stone. "What kind of game?" His voice was dubious.

Elissa hesitated, fighting the urge to hide. But there was so much she needed to know. She breathed slowly.

"It's called Five Questions," she said. "The Northern people play it. If you can guess what I am thinking after five questions, you get a prize.

73

It's easy," she finished. Actually, Five Questions could get positively dangerous. While valley children played it for fun, traders used it to wrest information from one another, which sometimes led to fistfights. And potential suitors played it to evaluate one another's feelings, which often led to embarrassment or heartache. Elissa preferred playing it with Gertrude or Cassius rather than Willie, who usually cheated, asking questions that had no relevance to the object of the game. He didn't have the interest or the attention span to play by the rules.

Falk leaned forward to pluck something that gleamed pale against the dark earth, and hid it in his tunic. "You ask the questions," he said. "A prize for my thought."

"You know this game?" asked Elissa, puzzled.

"Yes," said Falk. "Your mother taught it to me."

Elissa marveled at the words "your mother." Impulsively, she decided to follow Willie's example.

"What was her name?" Elissa asked. She held her breath. He *had* to answer. Those were the rules—even if she wasn't quite following them.

Falk looked taken aback, though he did not balk at the question.

"Galantha," he replied softly.

Her name was Galantha. Elissa held the name in her mouth like a pearl: *Galantha.* It was a perfect name for her mother—the first flower of spring, the snowdrop. She looked up to see that Falk's eyes were again upon her, but they were out of focus, looking into the past.

"She was green and white, like the flower," he said distantly. "Green eyes, white skin. Very delicate, almost translucent. She glowed." Realizing he was looking at Elissa's face, he returned to the present. For a moment Elissa thought he was going to caress her cheek, but he was merely trying to crush a small white moth that was fluttering around Elissa's face.

"Oh, no," she said, backing slightly away. "They do no harm."

Falk stiffened, rebuffed.

Elissa smiled reassuringly. "They often come at dusk." But he did not reach out again.

"You cheated," he said sternly. "You knew that wasn't what I was thinking. But I will give you that question for free. What is your next question?"

Elissa had a thousand questions. But Falk's expression, remote and cool, did not invite confidences. She realized that this was not the time to ask about her mother. It could wait. Elissa knew she would eventually find out what kind of mother she had—if not from him, then from someone among Falk's kin who had known her. Besides, the game demanded that she divine what was on Falk's mind, and there were surely more immediate matters occupying his thoughts.

"Where are we going, and why?"

Falk seemed to be prepared for this question. "The Citadel of the Khan," he answered. "We'll be making a stop along the way."

"The Citadel of the Khan!" Elissa found herself whispering. Falk looked at her with an odd, unreadable expression.

"He has invited us to visit." He held up two fingers. "By the way, that was two."

Elissa nodded. She didn't really believe she could get away with a double question. Falk was far too astute for that kind of trick. But the

76

Citadel of the Khan! Even farmers in High Crossing knew of the Citadel. The Khan's wealth was legendary, and his palace was reputed to be the finest in the world. However, very few travelers had actually seen the interior of the Khan's Citadel, as it was surrounded by a vast stretch of desert. She tapped her fingers lightly against her cheek, pensive. Now that she thought about it, she doubted that they were going to pay a social visit to a warlord accompanied, as they were, by a dozen armed soldiers. Elissa squinted at Falk. She might look like a child, but she did not appreciate being treated like one.

"Not a social visit," he amended. "This is more like a political visit."

Elissa was silent for a moment. "Who is that man, Kreel?"

"He was sent by the Khan to watch you." Falk looked down into his hands.

Elissa frowned. Why would the Khan need to watch her? She was just old Nana's orphan, no one of importance. She shook her head, denying her own thoughts. Not anymore, she reminded herself. She was no longer some simple country girl given up to be raised by the local healer. She was the daughter of a lord, and now her existence had value. But what kind?

"Why?" she asked. She was getting close.

"You"—Falk took a deep breath—"are going to win a war. That's four. One last question."

"Me? How?" Elissa exclaimed.

This final question was the one Falk had been saving his prize for. As it happened, he never had a chance to answer, because at that moment there was a clash of metal. Falk was up on his feet even before the shout burst forth from his lips.

"Run, Elissa! Back to your tent!"

Suddenly the woods erupted into a melee of soldiers and swords. It all happened so quickly, it seemed that time had come unhinged. Even before Falk shouted his command, Elissa was gone. Falk wasted not a moment but quickly dashed to Aldric, who was already battling several darkly swathed figures. One of the attackers launched himself directly at Falk. Falk spun and placed a sharp kick square in the man's solar plexus, knocking the attacker off course. A knife flew out of his hand, and Falk caught it neatly in midair. He turned to his opponent, positioning

78

himself for the counterattack. But the man was gone.

Ahead in the darkness Falk could just make out his own soldiers, who, being well trained by Aldric, were fiercely battling the hooded figures, jabbing at the dark shapes as they came spilling from the woods. The attackers seemed to be made of smoke for all the effect his soldiers had upon them. Wherever his men struck, the dark figures disappeared, only to reappear shortly afterward in a different spot. Falk cast a glance toward Elissa's tent to make sure the guards were still in position.

Then, as quickly as they had appeared, the dark shapes vanished, melting back into the woods. The camp went abruptly silent. Amazingly, it hardly looked as though a pitched battle had been fought only moments before. The soldiers looked a little dazed. Falk drew close to Aldric, who was unharmed though winded.

"Any casualties?" asked Falk.

"No, none that I know of," replied Aldric. "Should we follow?" Aldric was waiting for the command, holding his sword at the ready.

"No. It's too dark, and they have the advantage.

Did you manage to get a look at any of the brigands?"

Aldric shook his head. "Their faces were covered." He hesitated.

"Come out with it, man!" ordered Falk.

"They weren't thieves. They took nothing, and then they just vanished." Aldric continued to shake his head. "I've never seen anything like it."

"Perhaps our friend Kreel will know something about this," said Falk. "Go to his tent while I check on Elissa."

Rapidly, Falk made his way across the camp to Elissa's tent. The two guards rose unsteadily as Falk approached.

"Have you been wounded?" Falk asked.

"No, sir," they answered miserably.

Then, all at once, Falk understood. With one quick motion he thrust aside the tent flap and entered. The pallet was strewn with Elissa's possessions. She was not within.

"We never moved," said one of the guards, a tall youth. "We swear it."

Falk didn't waste time with reprimands. He'd deal with the guards later.

"Search the camp!" Falk barked. The soldiers scattered.

Aldric approached, his step heavy. "Kreel is gone," he said.

Falk clenched his fist. "Fool!" he muttered to himself. "I should have known that snake would pull something like this!"

"We will find her, my lord," promised Aldric. "They will not dare harm her."

"They had better not," said Falk ominously. He joined the search, but after combing the camp, corral, and nearby woods, Falk was forced to admit defeat. Elissa was nowhere to be found.

⤚ 5 ⤜

A Spirit

Elissa was in total darkness. Wildly she fought her captors, kicking and twisting, but it was no use. Her arms were securely pinned by a set of strong arms, and her head was covered in cloth. Even as she strained against them, one captor lifted her straight off the ground while another grabbed her feet. They carried her into the forest without making a sound.

"Help!" she cried, though it was just as useless to cry out as it was to struggle. By now she was too far away for Falk to hear her muffled cries.

All at once she heard a sharp thud. Instantly her feet were dropped. Another thud, and the man who held her arms grunted sharply and let go as well. Elissa tore off the hood and scrambled to her feet, only to run into a solid wall of animal hide.

"Always rushing," said a familiar voice.

"Gertrude!" exclaimed Elissa. "What are *you* doing here?"

"Never mind what *I'm* doing here," snorted Gertrude. "What are *you* doing here? This is no place for a young girl."

Elissa looked down at the ground, where two men were lying motionless. One of them was moaning softly.

"What did you *do* to them?" exclaimed Elissa.

"Bessie's not the only one who can land a kick," she said. "Too bad she cracked a hoof." The donkey craned her head around and examined her back foot. "Although I have to say, I've never been *that* good before."

One of the men stirred.

"Hop on," said Gertrude. "We'll go through the woods."

"But that's where *they* came from!" protested Elissa.

Gertrude cocked her ears forward. "Are you going to come with me? Or are you going to stand here and argue until these two hooligans wake up? Because if you are, I might as well—"

"All right!" Elissa clambered onto Gertrude's back without any further argument. Gertrude turned neatly and trotted into the forest, with Elissa holding her tightly around the neck.

The woods were as dark as pitch, and eerily silent. Elissa hoped that they were empty of the bandits who had tried to abduct her. She felt, rather than saw, the presence of the looming trees as the gloom enveloped them. Gertrude seemed to know where she was going, however, for she skirted the massive trunks with ease. The donkey made her way purposefully, as though she were on her way to breakfast.

"Gertrude," whispered Elissa, "where are we going?"

"We are going *away*," snorted Gertrude.

"But away where? How will we get back to camp?"

"I'll take care of that," said Gertrude. "Now ease up on my neck. I can hardly breathe."

Elissa loosened her grip and put her head against Gertrude's neck.

"She's all right," whispered Gertrude. "She's just scared."

"What was that?" asked Elissa, sitting up.

"Shh," replied Gertrude. "I'm not talking to you."

"Who are you talking to, then? It's as silent as a tomb out here—and almost as cold." Elissa was shaking violently.

"It's not cold. You've just had a fright," said Gertrude, not unkindly. "Now just hush and hold on."

Gertrude trotted straight through the dark forest, stopping only occasionally to avoid hummocks that had mounded up around fallen tree trunks. The rhythm of Gertrude's hooves made Elissa sleepy. Soon she was nodding to their steady beat as they tapped out her mother's name— *Galantha, Galantha, Galantha.* Perhaps she said the name aloud once or twice. She must have fallen asleep, for soon she dreamt she was beside Nana's fire with all the clay pots nestled in the embers like eggs about to hatch. Nana was saying, "Hotter, hotter, hotter..." Then Gertrude's sudden stop woke her up.

"We're here," Gertrude announced.

"Here" was a small clearing, at the center of which stood a hut. A pile of wood had been neatly stacked by the front door. An ax hung by the entrance. Elissa slid off Gertrude's back and, advancing on legs made wobbly from the long ride, raised her hand to knock on the stout wooden door.

"Nobody's home," said Gertrude. "You can go in."

"Come with me," said Elissa. "I'm not going in there by myself." She pulled the latchstring and entered, draping her arm around Gertrude's neck for support. The interior was composed of a single room, which Elissa noticed was clean and well kept. A fieldstone fireplace took up one whole wall. Elissa drew close to the hearth and, using a piece of kindling, poked at the coals. The stones were still slightly warm.

"Gertrude," she began somewhat hesitantly, "I don't think we should stay. Whoever made this fire might be back at any moment. We don't know what kind of person lives here. . . ." She didn't finish the thought; the image of dark figures spilling out of the woods was still fresh in her mind.

Gertrude had already lain down before the hearth.

"Nobody's here," she yawned. "Let's go to sleep."

Within a few moments Gertrude's steady snoring filled the room. Elissa tried to wonder how Gertrude knew so much, but she couldn't hold the thought. Her mind did not want to work. Exhausted, she curled up beside Gertrude's comforting bulk and was soon asleep herself.

While Elissa lay in slumber beside Gertrude's warm flank, Falk and Aldric passed the night conferring in tense whispers. Falk's soldiers had taken up their habitual round of night shifts, though even they realized the futility of their watch. If the attackers wished to make a second assault, they could appear, do their damage, and vanish again into the forest without a trace, much as they had done only hours before. Falk, however, was not concerned about a second attack. He believed the attackers had gotten what they came for.

"What do you think, Aldric?" Falk paced as he talked.

Aldric stood to one side, examining the curve of the knife Falk had confiscated.

"What is it?" asked Falk.

"Something isn't right. There were hoofprints all around Elissa's tent. Yet there were no signs of animals anywhere else. Our attackers came on foot."

"One of the horses?" asked Falk.

"No," said Aldric. "They are donkey tracks."

"A donkey?" Falk stopped pacing for a moment, his forehead creased in puzzlement. "It makes no sense."

"No, it doesn't," said Aldric. "She was not taken by bandits. The thieves and cutthroats who inhabit this forest have absolutely no need for donkeys, outside of eating them." Aldric held up the knife. "And the men who carried these knives would not have traveled with a donkey, either."

"Who does that leave?" asked Falk. "Kreel?"

"It's possible Kreel could have taken her," said Aldric. "But he'd have to be traveling on foot. He certainly did not have a donkey hidden away."

Falk struck his fist against his palm, exasperated. "Well, Kreel is gone and *someone* took her!

She wasn't abducted by spirits!" He sat down and rubbed his forehead. "The question is, what do we do now?"

"We could proceed to the rendezvous," said Aldric. "Without Elissa."

"We'd have no bargaining power," Falk replied tersely. "Without her we have nothing. Elissa was supposed to be a guarantee against a loan. If I don't hand her over, the Khan has no reason to lend me any troops at all."

Aldric sat down heavily. "This was a bad idea to begin with."

"Yes, I know, you've told me. But it was the *only* idea," interjected Falk.

Aldric cocked an eye at Falk. "Surely not," he said.

"You know full well the Khan would not accept a promise to pay. I suppose giving my word wasn't enough for him." Falk spoke stiffly. He was a noble, and his word was his bond.

Aldric stood. "Well, if you insist on following this course of action, we could stay and look for her. By day we will surely find a trail."

"Then we will be late, and if the Khan leaves

the rendezvous point, we'll never find the Citadel on our own." Falk had risen to his feet and was pacing angrily. "I'll lose my kingdom!"

Aldric shook his head. "I don't suppose you explained any of this to Elissa."

"Not yet," said Falk. "I was about to present my position to her when we were attacked."

"No doubt," said Aldric dryly. "Do you think she would have understood it?"

A thoughtful expression came over Falk's face. "She's not as slow as I first thought," he said. "I'm sure she'd have understood." Falk fell silent as an idea formed in his mind. "Aldric, how fast can you travel?"

"Alone?"

"With an archer," said Falk.

Aldric immediately grasped Falk's plan.

"Very fast, my lord. There is no track I can't follow."

"Good. If you can catch up with them, we may have a chance," said Falk.

"Yes," Aldric agreed. "Whether it's Kreel or raiders, we'll be able to pick them off before they know what hit them. We'll find her, my lord."

"You'll leave at dawn," said Falk. "And when you have found her, meet us at the rendezvous."

When Aldric left the tent a few moments later, he was not entirely sure the plan would succeed. It seemed laden with uncertainties to him. Nevertheless, at dawn he departed with his best archer. As he left camp, he glanced briefly through Falk's tent flap. Falk was still seated just as Aldric had left him, gazing into his hand at a limp white flower.

The floor was hard and cold under Elissa's head. *I've rolled off my mattress,* she thought. Then, as she recalled where she was, and how she had gotten there, she sat up with a start. Gertrude was gone! She was alone! For the first time since she was a small child, Elissa felt afraid of the dark. Crunching noises, like the movement of stealthy feet on dry leaves, came from outside the hut. Her hand crept out toward the fireplace, searching for a stick, a log, a rock, anything she could use to defend herself. She was fumbling around in the ashes when the door opened with a crash. The morning light streamed in through the doorway.

91

"Breakfast!" announced Gertrude with a happy swish of her tail. Her mouth was stuffed with grass. "What are you doing with that stick?"

Elissa put her makeshift weapon down. "Don't do that!" she cried.

"Do what?" asked Gertrude, chewing.

"Don't sneak up on me again!"

Gertrude snorted and swished her tail. "Donkeys don't *sneak*," she said. "We leave that to you two-legged folks." She tossed her head and backed away from the door.

Elissa slumped by the cold hearth. She shouldn't have yelled at Gertrude like that. After all, if it weren't for Gertrude, she'd still be in the hands of those men. Elissa shuddered.

She gazed about, examining the interior of the hut. Her impression last night had been that it was quite bare. But in the morning light she could see that it possessed several pieces of simple furniture. A small wooden cupboard was located next to the hearth, alongside of which was placed a rough-hewn table and single chair. There was a platform that probably served as a bed along the opposite wall. It looked very much as though the hut was the dwelling of a sole occupant. A hermit. *Well,* she told herself, *hermits are generally harmless.* She only hoped that when this one returned, he wouldn't be too upset at the intrusion. Elissa picked herself up and turned her thoughts to breakfast.

First she started a fire, using a piece of flint that she discovered in a chink in the chimney stones. Rummaging through the cupboard, Elissa found a tin of crushed oats, a clay pot, and a wooden bowl and spoon. She tossed a handful of crushed oats into the pot and poured in some water from a jug that stood nearby. Within a few minutes the oats were bubbling merrily on the fire. She added a drop of honey, which she found in a crock by the table.

As she stirred the pot, she tried to piece together the events of the previous evening. She'd heard the clash of metal. Simultaneously, a small voice, right in her ear, had said "Fly!" The voice had sparked such a feeling of panic in her that she had stood up and started to run. Then her father had shouted for her to run to her tent, but before she had reached it, a pair of arms had grabbed her out of nowhere, yanked a hood over her head, and dragged her into the woods. The sounds of clashing swords and shouting were terrible. Then Gertrude . . .

How did Gertrude find me? Where am I? How did we get here? Questions began to swarm in Elissa's head like gnats. *Why did those men try to kidnap me? How am I going to win a war? How am I going to get back to camp?* The more she thought about her circumstances, the more the questions arose. Nobody *ever* explained anything to her—certainly not Nana. And now her father! He hadn't explained anything, either. Elissa's head hurt.

I need to eat, she thought.

She emptied the oatmeal into the wooden bowl and dipped in her spoon. The first bite was heavenly. She finished the bowl rapidly.

And what *of* her father?

At the thought of Falk, Elissa fell deeply into confusion. She didn't understand him. After thirteen years of being virtually dead, at least to her, he had appeared out of nowhere. He had taken her away from her home, Nana, everything she knew. Elissa slumped. If she was important to him, then why had he waited so long to find her?

"Perhaps I wasn't worth looking for," she whispered.

94

The small fire was nearly out. She scattered the coals listlessly with a stick. How could she be expected to figure this out by herself?

What does he expect of me? she wondered. In the short time they'd been together, she'd done everything a good daughter was supposed to do. She'd been patient, obedient, kind; and if he'd let her, she'd be loving. But he hadn't seemed to want any of those things from her. All she knew was that she was lost, deep in the heart of this wilderness.

Elissa slowly rose to her feet. At least she had Gertrude. She walked to the door, already dreading the sight of those dark, forbidding trees. But she needed to see somebody familiar right now, someone who was part of her old life. In the open doorway, however, she stopped short, arrested in mid-step. Silvery rays fell in straight, brilliant beams between the tree trunks, like pillars. They illuminated the glade with a clear, soft light. The early morning mist floated in drifts above the grass, which sparkled where the sun struck the fine strands of spiderwebs. Gertrude stood in the center of the clearing, grazing. A moth flitted lazily around her drooping ears. Elissa held her breath, not wishing to disturb the complete peace of the moment.

She felt her heart swell with the beauty and mystery of the world. She took a step forward onto the dew-laden grass, taking in the serenity of the forest with wide eyes and an open heart. And in that moment the forest underwent a transformation. The trees, which had at first looked so sinister to her, now appeared as faithful sentinels guarding her door. She took in a deep breath of the sweet forest air, drawing it down into the center of her being. It was like a magic elixir. She sensed the deep subterranean connection, the belonging, the peace. The forest flowed up through her, vibrating in her bones, shaking every fiber of her body with its deep thrum. Elissa felt rooted to the earth. She couldn't have moved if she had tried, nor did she want to. There was something hovering right on the edge of her awareness, something whispering a message to her soul. *This is yours,* it said. Then it was gone, leaving in its wake a girl standing thunderstruck in the dawn.

Elissa looked up at the treetops and then straightened herself up as tall as she could. A thrill of pure elation spread out from her chest and radiated through her body, erasing her doubts in its wake. She was Elissa, daughter of a lord. From now on she would act like one.

"Well," she called out cheerily, "are you going to tell me?"

Gertrude, who had ambled up to the door hoping for a few oats to round out breakfast, looked as surprised as a donkey can look. "Tell you what?"

"You can start by telling me how you found me," she said.

Gertrude shifted uncomfortably from hoof to hoof.

"It's like this," she began. "I was standing in the pasture, eating some truly scrumptious clovers— you know, the ones with the purple flowers and the juicy leaves. . . ."

Elissa started packing up the oats. Gertrude hurried to finish.

"Somebody told me to get going. So I went. It was easy enough to follow your trail."

"That's it?" exclaimed Elissa in disbelief. "Somebody said 'go' and you *went*?" For a beast of Gertrude's renowned stubbornness, she had been remarkably cooperative when a perfect stranger had said "giddyup." Who could he have been, then? Elissa must have been talking out loud, because Gertrude answered her.

"*She*, I think," said Gertrude, without certainty. "It was a very small kind of voice."

Elissa was finally piecing it all together. "I do believe we have a fairy, or a pixie," she said. Elissa looked up at the trees. "Or perhaps it's a spirit," she murmured.

"Oh, yes," replied Gertrude, munching on the oats Elissa held in her hand. "These are good."

Elissa wiped her hands on her skirt. "Gertrude, if you can pay attention for just a moment longer, did the voice tell you anything else?"

Gertrude flicked her ears, annoyed at all the interruptions. "It told me to hurry—which I did. If you will recall, I *did* rescue you." Gertrude swished her tail modestly. "And it told me how to get here."

"Did it tell you how to get back to camp?"

Gertrude's mouth was full, so she merely nodded her head toward the west—away from the valley and Castlemar.

"Well," said Elissa briskly, "Nana always said 'He who will not follow the fates will be dragged by them.' West it is." There were obviously higher forces at work here, which, for the time being, she would have to trust. In any event, the spirit probably meant her no harm. After all, it had brought her to the safety of the hermit's glen. She had no doubt it would eventually take her back to her father as well. Elissa smiled to herself, for now she had a goal. She would earn Falk's respect—and perhaps, eventually, his love.

Before she left the hermit's hut, Elissa placed Nana's little tin of salve in the wooden cupboard. The hermit was more deserving than Kreel, she told herself, and could probably make better use of it. In any case, it was a fitting exchange for the peace of mind she had found in this tranquil glade. Then, without further thought, she climbed on Gertrude's back, setting out through the green-leafed columns of the forest chapel and into the new day. She had dreamt of traveling the world to find her father, hadn't she? There was no better time to start than the present.

6

Bargaining Chip

Khoonbish, the fourth Khan of the Southern Desert, Master of the High Steppes, and aspiring Emperor of the World, sat alone in his tent, playing War against himself. His mother had named him Khoonbish—*Not a Person*—in an attempt to keep evil spirits from noticing him at birth. It was especially important that her child not attract the attention of evil spirits, for he was the son of a Khan and liable to stand out in many ways. As it happens, her ploy failed. The spirits found Khoonbish, and no amount of distraction could keep them from him. On the day Khoonbish became Khan, he banished his name, along with several hundred subjects who had happened to displease him. These days only his mother dared call him by his given name. To the rest of the world, he was simply: the Khan.

The tent that housed the Khan reflected the stature, and tastes, of its occupant. Deep-piled rugs lay one upon another, their jewel-like colors gleaming vibrantly in the diffuse light. Countless pillows, ottomans, and embroidered cushions adorned the carpets in soft mounds. One of these mounds was the Khan himself, who was garbed in the same rich colors as the dozen cushions with which his servants had propped up his enormous body. The Khan had discovered long ago that propping himself up was best achieved through the efforts of others.

As he contemplated his next move, the Khan looked up, perhaps to gain inspiration from his forefathers, whose glorious exploits were depicted on the tapestries that covered the tent walls. The history of the previous Khans had been permanently recorded on cloth so that their fierce mustaches, their proud bearing, and the noble deeds they had performed in battle would always provide a model for future Khans. They surrounded him now, their hands grasping swords, their expressions implacable and, as they looked down at him, somewhat disappointed. It was as if they somehow knew, even as they were being embroidered for posterity, that the current Khan would never live up to their standards. The Khan frowned. Not for him the cold nights spent tossing and turning on some bleak expanse of uncomfortable rock, the dawn marches, the uninteresting food, the lack of entertainment. He believed in taking his comforts with him. If and when the Khan overcame his enemies, it would be through subterfuge, not strength. And while the old Khans might have disapproved of his methods, he knew that, in the end, victory was all that mattered.

The Khan looked away from the harsh stares of his ancestors, banishing these tiresome reminders of tradition with his next bold, and probably illegal, move. He held the black knight suspended over the board. He could take the white queen—that would be satisfying. Or he could take a pawn and put the white king in check. Also satisfying. However, both would be even better. The tiny garnet eyes of the knight gleamed up at him. The Khan smiled and captured the white queen, then captured the pawn, placing her king in check. He yawned. Then he leaned luxuriously back into his cushions, patting his broad middle. The Khan loved the prospect of winning. It was so pleasant, so relaxing, so soothing. . . .

Two sharp claps disturbed the Khan's intended nap. *Blast these disturbances,* he thought. He wondered if he should behead a few of his guards, just to remind them that a man should not be kept from his rest. Fortunately for the guards, his initial annoyance was soon replaced by happy anticipation. This must be the news he'd been waiting for! *My prize will soon be within my grasp,* he thought, *and with it a highly strategic kingdom to add to my empire.* The Khan licked his lips and called out his permission to enter.

"Ah, Kreel," exclaimed the Khan. "I have been waiting. What have you brought me?"

Kreel made a bow of the sort that the Khan expected and appreciated, deep and long. It won Kreel a little time. Not enough, unfortunately, for while he was still bent over, the tent flap was thrust aside and the leader of the raiding party entered the tent, accompanied by two young warriors. They stood there in their deep blue robes for just a moment too long. Then they made brief, perfunctory bows, the sort that irritated the Khan. The desert tribesmen were much too independent for the Khan's tastes.

Ah, but what fighters they were! They were swift and silent as raptors descending for the kill, and just as deadly. There was no army in the world that could match them for courage and skill, for in other lands most soldiers were nothing but farmers. It was said that when a boy was born in the desert, the midwife cut the cord that bound him to his mother with a sword. Yes, when it came right down to it, the Khan had to admit that the Blue People were his most valuable resource. Through them he not only controlled all caravan routes, he possessed an impregnable desert fortress—the Citadel—the route to which the Blue People guarded jealously. It was fortunate that his great-grandfather had married into their line, guaranteeing several generations of allegiance.

Backward creatures, he thought. *But allegiances are very useful. As are wives.* The Khan lingered on that thought.

Kreel, who was familiar with the Khan's mental journeys, was keeping very still and silent, in hopes that the Khan would forget his presence entirely. The untimely appearance of the tribesmen had complicated matters a bit. He wouldn't be able to lie as easily. If only the Khan would remain preoccupied for a few moments longer, he was almost sure that he could sneak out the way he had come in. Kreel began to inch backward. Regrettably, the Khan returned from his mental rambles all too soon.

"Well? Speak up!" he demanded. "Where is she?"

"O Great and Noble Khan," Kreel began, speaking with his head still bent toward the floor. "We have met with an unforeseen and entirely unpreventable setback."

"*What?*" cried the Khan, deeply enraged. He struggled among the unresisting cushions. "Idiots, dolts, donkeys!" he shouted. "A fool's errand! Your grandmother could have done better! Your grandmother *has* done better! How dare you return alive! You have ruined all my plans!"

While the Khan searched in vain among his cushions for a sword, his rage abated, for his mind had begun to be pleasantly occupied with the thought of killing Kreel in many entertaining fashions. The Khan stopped rummaging as his mind roamed, leaving Kreel suspended in mid-bow. The spy prayed silently and contemplated his perhaps woefully short future. Behind him one of the tribesmen shifted uncomfortably on his feet, not quite praying but equally as fearful, for his grandmother was not a woman to be trifled with. He hoped the Khan wouldn't tell her.

"My Khan," wheezed Kreel, "the attack went as planned, but the girl—"

"The girl is a demon!" interrupted one of the young tribesmen. "Before our very eyes she transformed herself into a beast." As the Khan was not regarding him in any manner resembling sympathy, the young man faltered. "She had glowing green eyes, and hooves—sharp as knives—and she struck us so." He displayed the devastation of the "demon's" hooves upon his own bruised face and torso. Kreel straightened slightly, looking back over his hunched shoulders with a glimmer of hope in his eyes. Maybe he would escape with his life after all—if the blame could be shifted onto these desert folk. He glanced at the Khan.

Ah, good. The Khan was no longer looking in his direction but at the tribesmen. "What is this child babbling about?" the Khan demanded of the leader. "Account for yourself!"

The man looked briefly at his younger companions and then shook his head. "My Khan," he said carefully, "this girl, this child you have sent us to fetch, is not as she appears. There is a curse on the man who would harm her. So our Om Chai has spoken."

The Khan was tempted to laugh but restrained himself. *These Blue People and their superstitions!* he thought. Next thing he knew, they'd be saying their beasts had spoken! However, these men were not cowards. If their soothsayer had issued a warning, then there must be a reason. There was always a reason, and the Khan would discover it before long. All rumors came to his palace, and all knowledge could be bought. He could afford to be patient, for in the end he would have her. The Khan always got what he wanted. Getting what he wanted was a very pleasant thought, one he often lingered on. But not now, not here. If he could not steal her now, he would steal her later. The Khan looked at the white queen he still held between two sausagelike fingers. The girl was nearly within his grasp, just a few more moves.

"I will not kill you . . . yet," he said generously, holding his arms out wide to demonstrate his expansive nature and goodwill. "The girl is obviously protected by a djinn. But I am sure that if you treat her and her companions cordially, the desert spirit will not harm you. After you have taken them, and have offered them your hospitality, bring them to me. All except the soldiers." Having Falk brought to the Citadel would alter his plans slightly, but with only Falk and perhaps an advisor to deal with, he could still cheat at the game, no matter how well his opponents played. He gestured for the men to leave. At this they departed, Kreel first, with obvious relief, the desert men following soon after.

"Old camel fart," one of the youths muttered under his breath in the desert tongue. The elder man held back a smile. He agreed with his son's assessment of the Khan, though he would not voice it—yet. Soon enough their day would come. So their Om Chai had spoken.

At the edge of the wilderness the earth dropped abruptly away in a long, high ridge that resembled the first step of a gigantic stairway. Beneath it spread the vast plain of the high desert. When Falk reached the top, it became clear that there would be no meeting with the Khan. There was no sign of the Khan's party, or of Aldric. As Falk sat on his horse, gazing out over the barren landscape, he tallied his losses. He had lost Elissa and, along with her, his kingdom. He might have lost Aldric as well. The bitterness of defeat felt like a cold, hard knot in his stomach, which he could contain only by focusing on the vacant horizon. Falk sat silently on his horse for so long that his men grew restless. He felt them shifting behind him but did not turn. He was about to give the command to head back in the direction they had just come from when he saw a lone hawk drifting high above the desert floor. It circled casually once, twice, then with a scream dropped like a stone to the ground. When it arose, it held a small struggling creature in its talons. Falk took heart. Perhaps there was more to be gained in this empty expanse than he realized. He gave the order, and within moments he was leading his men down the steep path to the plain below.

As they descended, the air became drier and the view clearer. The foreshortening effect of great height diminished as they approached the desert floor, and what had first seemed an empty plain now took on contour and details. Bumps became small wrinkled hills, their sides blotched with scrubby vegetation. A group of what appeared to be several dozen dark boulders dotted the landscape in an odd semicircle. For the most part these were small and rounded, resembling from a distance a game of marbles that had been left unfinished.

As Falk and his men approached the desert floor, he realized that these boulders were not part of the natural landscape. The rocks twisted and stretched themselves into thin columns. Then, in the blink of an eye, they bore weapons. Within seconds Falk and his party were surrounded. Falk gave a small sign to his men to sheathe their arms. He turned to address the dark figures that stood silently around them. The dark men did not reply but merely nudged Falk's horses, moving them toward the base of the ridge. Falk decided there was no point in offering resistance.

The group proceeded in silence. The only sounds were the steady *clop, clop* of the horses' hooves and the soft swishing of desert robes. Ahead, Falk made out the shape of a tent. Then another seemed to spring from the soil. And another. He stared until, finally, he saw an entire village of dun-colored tents. Their color had so perfectly matched the dull browns and grays of the surrounding desert that they were impossible to identify from a distance. The tents were surrounded by another circle of dark mounds. Falk felt a small stirring of anxiety.

Falk's men made their approach slowly and deliberately, weaving their way carefully between the thorny plants that seemed to spread over every square inch of the rocky plain. Falk rode a little ahead of the rest of his men, considering his options. There were none. As they neared the encampment, the path widened and more dark figures appeared. They held curved knives.

"Greetings," cried Falk. He held up both hands to show he bore no weapon.

The tall men did not move, but one of the dark shapes separated itself from the rest and moved forward. It was difficult to make out whether this person was old or young, man or woman, as it was swathed from head to toe. All wore dark blue robes, the characteristic midnight blue of the desert tribes that occupied the huge expanse of desert buffering the Khan's territory to the south. The tribes had been forced to pledge allegiance to the previous Khan and to his father and grandfather before him. They now served the present Khan.

The figure strode to within a few feet of Falk's horse and then lifted one hand to remove the long veil that served to protect both face and head from the scorching desert sun. Underneath the cloth was a gray-haired man with the deeply etched face of an elder tribesman. In spite of the difference in height between them, it seemed the man on foot gazed directly into Falk's eyes.

"Welcome," said the man formally in Common Tongue, extending both palms before him in a time-honored gesture. "You are my guests."

With that short statement he turned and led Falk's party into the encampment. More dark figures silently emerged to take their horses and tend to them. Falk was ushered into the largest of the tents by two armed guards. Though their desert garb hid the bottom parts of their faces from him, Falk noted that their unwavering gazes did not look especially welcoming, in spite of the leader's greeting. The swords they gripped across their chests glinted threateningly in the sun. But once the leader had admitted them as guests, no member of the tribe would harm them. Or so he hoped.

Falk entered the tent expecting to find the leader and his sons. Instead, there was only one figure sitting amid the cushions and rugs that covered the tent floor.

"Aldric!" he cried.

In two strides Falk closed the distance between them, though as Aldric rose to make his greeting, Falk could see that his plans for negotiation would have to be abandoned. From the slump of Aldric's shoulders and the dullness in his eyes, Falk knew that his mission had not been successful. He gestured for him to sit. Aldric might have preferred the formality of making his report while standing, but Falk felt altogether tired—weary to the bone, in fact.

"Tell me," he said.

"I have failed, my lord," said Aldric without preamble. It was to Aldric's credit that he never offered any excuses. Aldric took all his duties and responsibilities personally. It was for that reason, in part, that Falk had come to trust him so completely. He nodded to Aldric to continue.

"The trail the attackers took led us due west, parallel to the forest road." Aldric stopped briefly, collecting his thoughts. "However, the donkey's trail led north. We could not follow both."

Falk waited silently. He knew the outcome of Aldric's decision.

"It was more likely that the attackers had taken Elissa than that a donkey had, and so we followed them here," Aldric continued. "The Khan had not yet left. He broke camp shortly after we arrived. Kreel was with him. Alone."

Falk rose to his feet, suddenly not tired at all. "They don't have Elissa!" He began to pace. Aldric cleared his throat. There was more.

"Go on," Falk bade him continue.

"We were captured before we could return." Aldric stopped in embarrassment. "It was much like the previous raid. We did not hear them until they were nearly upon us."

Aldric waited for a rebuke, but Falk, busy with his own thoughts, was clearly elsewhere. He spun on his heels, his mind buzzing. "He doesn't have her. So he must believe she is still with us! Where in blazes is she?"

Falk continued his restless pacing while Aldric waited. At one point he struck his palm against his forehead as if to jar his mind into action. Then a thought came to mind, one that stopped him in his tracks. He looked at Aldric thoughtfully.

"She could very well have set out on her own, Aldric," he said.

"My lord," Aldric protested, "a helpless young girl would not set off alone, at night, unprotected, in such dangerous territory. . . ." Noting Falk's expression, he let the thought trail off.

"You know *I* would have," said Falk.

"Like father, like daughter," mumbled Aldric under his breath.

Falk stopped pacing to face Aldric squarely.

"The Khan doesn't have her, but neither do we. And although we entered this desert camp easily enough, I suspect it will not be quite as easy to leave. Therefore we cannot go back to find her."

"No," agreed Aldric. "The Khan left these men to wait for you here. I believe they were supposed to act as escorts for Elissa. The question is, *why?* What purpose would abducting Elissa serve? He would have had her anyway as his guarantee."

"Yes, and I would have had his troops. That was our agreement. But if he had stolen Elissa and had her directly transported to his Citadel, he could have feigned ignorance of her whereabouts and refused me his troops when we met here. Oh, he is a devious one! He never intended to give me his troops to begin with!"

Aldric nodded. "And at such a distance from the Citadel, we would not have been able to search for her. With Elissa as a hostage, he could have pressured you into anything."

"Yes." Falk's eyes hardened. "He might even have aided my enemies." Falk breathed deeply and sat next to Aldric. "But now the Khan doesn't know what to do. Now that his plan to kidnap

Elissa has failed, his course of action has become limited."

"What do you propose?" asked Aldric.

Falk looked up, as if searching for an answer. "Nothing," he said. "Unfortunately, we are also at an impasse. Without Elissa I have no bargaining power. There is little point in continuing with this endeavor."

Aldric waited for Falk to finish—to propose a plan of action, or request one. Falk did not speak but sat calmly contemplating the roof of the tent.

Aldric squinted at Falk, puzzled. "You don't seem upset, my lord. Are you rethinking your plan?"

Falk remained silent for several moments more before he turned his eyes back to Aldric. "I wonder if perhaps you haven't been right all along," he said finally. "This may have been a bad idea. And not just because of the necessity for this agreement." Falk closed his eyes, searching for words. "I think I would rather have an honorable defeat than an ignoble victory. Using Elissa as a bargaining chip was—"

As Falk spoke, a shaft of light penetrated the

dim interior of the tent. A strange beast entered and planted its front hooves sturdily on the rug. A slender figure stood beside it, one arm flung over its neck, the other holding back the tent flap.

"Who is using me as a bargaining chip?" Elissa demanded.

7

Reins of Power

Elissa stood in the entrance to the tent, allowing her eyes to adjust. Her abrupt appearance had halted Falk in mid-sentence. He looked at her, his mouth slightly open. It was Aldric, however, who uttered the first words.

"The donkey!" he exclaimed.

"Gertrude," corrected Elissa.

Gertrude nodded gravely to the men, who sat stunned before her. Automatically the two men nodded back. Neither one could devise a better response.

Elissa patted the donkey on her shoulder. It was time for Gertrude to leave. She wished she could say a word of farewell to her, but Gertrude, unlike people, understood Elissa's feelings without needing constant reaffirmation. Gertrude turned and ambled away with a snort that was more eloquent than words.

"How did you get here?" asked Falk.

"We walked," explained Elissa. "Through the woods." Then, when Falk remained silent, she added, "Gertrude carried me some of the way." There was nothing else to say. The donkey had simply followed the trail left by her father until she'd reached the desert camp. There had been no guards, of course, as Falk and his men had already been captured. "It was very pleasant," she said. And it had been—until now.

Aldric and Falk exchanged glances.

Elissa looked from one man to the other, hesitating. Then she gathered up her newfound sense of purpose and forged ahead. "Well," she repeated, "who is using me as a bargaining chip?" To her surprise, and apparently theirs as well, she had no intention of backing down.

"I am," Falk said. "Or I was."

Falk patted the cushion beside him as an invitation for her to sit. Aldric cleared his throat and shifted uneasily. Then he rose to his feet.

"I think I'll go join Gertrude," he said. And with that he made his exit.

Elissa sat beside Falk. She was not completely sure what a "bargaining chip" was, but judging from Aldric's rapid retreat and Falk's obvious discomfort, she suspected it was something bad. Elissa was beginning to feel a curious sensation in her chest. She arranged her skirts and forced herself to stay put.

"This might not make much sense to you," Falk began. "But at this moment I am not sure myself that anything I have done in the past thirteen years makes much sense. Sometimes it all seems so . . . unnecessary." He hesitated.

Elissa did not move. She was waiting for the truth.

"You see," he continued, "when I was a young man, my whole life had already been planned for me. I was to marry the daughter of a neighboring lord, a man with lands and wealth and power. The arrangements had been made before I was born. Of course I had never seen the girl; our families did not consider that to be important. What was important to them was the joining of forces, the consolidation of power. I was simply a means to an end. Just as you were intended to be, Elissa."

Elissa didn't understand how "means to an end" applied to her. But it was not yet time for her to speak. That time would come. Falk looked uncomfortable. He continued his tale. "My father believed that a firsthand knowledge of the workings of the silk trade would stand me in good stead, since the majority of his holdings were devoted to the production of silk. So he sent me to all the markets, from High Crossing to Alhamazar. After visiting the markets, I was to return to be married. My father had everything planned. I was his sole heir, and it was my duty."

"You are an only child?" asked Elissa.

Falk stopped his tale, somewhat puzzled at Elissa's question. "Yes," he said. "So was my father."

"Ah." Elissa breathed a little sigh of disappointment.

"Fourteen years ago my father decided to send me to the summer fair in High Crossing," continued Falk. "That's where I met your mother. Her tribe had come down from the Northern Waste to trade furs."

"From the North?" asked Elissa, perplexed. "You mean she was a nomad?" Elissa had never imagined her mother to be from the Northern tribes.

"Yes, she was the daughter of a chieftain."

Falk faltered for a moment, remembering. He looked directly into Elissa's eyes as if seeing them for the first time. "Galantha was an angel. She was my life. I could not help but love her. It wasn't anything I could control—or anything my father could control. At the end of the summer I did not return to Castlemar. Instead, I married her. In secret." Falk stopped for a moment and breathed. "We were happy. A few months later I returned home, alone, to make arrangements for Galantha to join me. That was my mistake—at least, one of them. I thought I could convince my father to accept Galantha into his household." Falk laughed bitterly. "I honestly believed it would be an easy task. She was so beautiful and so . . . pure. But as far as my father was concerned, a nomad was no better than a savage."

Elissa listened to Falk carefully. This was the story she had always wanted to hear, the story of a man and a woman who had conceived her in love. And yet, watching Falk's radiant face as he described the beauty of his Galantha, her purity, his undying love, she knew how Falk's love story would end. The light was already fading from his face.

"I never imagined the price I would have to pay for my disobedience. My father ordered his guards to throw me into Castlemar's dungeons until I renounced my marriage. I wouldn't. It was only due to Aldric's intervention that he did not leave me there to rot. But the old tyrant had thought of something better. He was plotting to have her murdered." Falk's voice shook.

Elissa looked at Falk with sudden comprehension. This was it. His true story was not about the love of his life—it was about hatred. And it hadn't ended. All these years had done nothing to temper his rage. Looking into Falk's stony eyes, she knew beyond question that her existence had not even made a dent in his armor. Elissa looked down at her hands. She picked up a pillow and held it against her stomach.

"When Aldric told me of my father's plan, I wanted to kill him," said Falk. "Unfortunately, I was confined to my quarters, so there was little I could do other than send Galantha a warning. I was so young, so foolish. I thought she could flee to safety. She attempted to return to the Northern Waste, to her father's encampment, but the winter was harsh that year. After a week in the snows, she returned to High Crossing, but traveling had weakened her; she was never very strong. She died in childbirth. So in the end it was my foolishness that killed her, not my father's cruelty."

Elissa found herself speaking. "When did you learn of my birth?" she asked.

"While I was in prison. The midwife sent me the news through a silk trader."

Elissa's head felt a little light, and her cheeks tingled. This was the truth she had been waiting for. Yes, Nana had known everything all along. But so had Falk. Elissa could remain silent, or face him.

"Why didn't you come for me?" Elissa said, in a voice so low it was nearly a whisper.

"It was for your own safety," said Falk. "If my father had known where you were, he would have had you killed. I had to protect you."

Falk wasn't telling the whole truth, and Elissa knew it. Falk had not renounced his daughter in order to save her. He was protecting himself from the pain of his own emptiness. Elissa could see it in his closed face, his shuttered eyes, the bitterness in his voice. When his love had died, she had taken his soul with her. And not even Galantha's daughter, his only child, could bring it back. "Conceived in love" does not mean "welcomed into the world." Elissa pressed her palms against her knees. Her resolve was dwindling fast.

"One simply cannot plan life," continued Falk. "The gods take great delight in foiling our designs. After my father had given up all hope of pressuring me into a marriage, and you had safely passed through your infancy, I thought you might join me. But I was faced with a drought, a failing kingdom, and an invasion." Falk gave a short, harsh laugh and shook his head. But Elissa didn't respond. She was waiting for the end of the story, his and hers.

"The drought had reduced our silk production down to a fraction of what it once was. And since we had already suffered such a mighty blow at Nature's hands, one of my rivals to the south decided this would be the ideal time to challenge my father's failing rulership." Falk shrugged, somewhat apologetically. "Family jealousies are always the worst."

The tale had taken an odd twist. Elissa was confused. "I thought you said one of your 'rivals.'"

"Yes," replied Falk. "A distant cousin, Gavin, Duke of Cardys. He is amassing troops near Castlemar's southern border. Apparently two of my other less consequential cousins have joined him."

"Your cousins?" Elissa was horrified. "They would attack their own family?"

"Of course," said Falk. "Who else? Eastern nobles are all family one way or another."

Elissa could not take it all in. A father who imprisoned his own son, who plotted the murder of his son's wife, and who would even murder his grandchild was something beyond her scope. Her own grandfather had wanted to kill her! Her cousins waged war on one another! What kind of a family was this?

Falk saw the blank expression on Elissa's face and misinterpreted it as doubt.

"Elissa, these sorts of disputes are common when men of position grow old, all the more so when they refuse to release the reins of power. While Gavin prepares for an invasion, my father sits doddering by the fire, recounting his days of glory. And there are rumors of a new kind of weapon, which could be devastating for us. Now, I don't know if Gavin possesses any of these weapons, but even if he doesn't, we are not in any kind of position to win a war. We need an ally. And that is where you come in."

Elissa was frowning deeply, trying to place herself in this strange story, trying to determine what any of this had to do with being a "bargaining chip."

"I don't see how I can play a part in all this," she said at last. "I certainly can't raise an army for you."

"Yes, you can," Falk countered. "The Khan hires out mercenaries, and very fine warriors they are indeed. He has also promised me a loan to help cover the soldiers' upkeep until I win the war."

"But don't you have your own soldiers?" Elissa did not understand the complexities of war, but she knew that each kingdom possessed an army.

"Each one of the Khan's warriors is worth ten of our recruits. Aldric trains his men well, but in the end they are still farmers. Believe me, we need help." He hesitated. "The Khan has agreed to place his troops at our disposal—on one condition. He wants a guarantee that I will pay back the loan. He somehow discovered you were in High Crossing." Falk frowned. "I don't know how he found out about you," he admitted.

Once again, Elissa was caught off guard. "You mean the Khan knew about me? He knew where I was?"

Falk looked away. "Yes. He specifically asked for my heir as a guarantee. By sheer coincidence, the midwife—your Nana—sent word shortly afterward, telling me where you were. I'd just assumed that you'd been taken to the North by my wife's family."

Elissa closed her eyes. This was too much for her to sort out. There were too many secrets, too many coincidences, too many *betrayals* for her to absorb what Falk was saying.

Falk continued speaking. "So you see, I am in a predicament. I need the Khan, and the Khan wants the princess—as security."

"But what does that have to do with me?" Elissa asked. "I'm just . . . just a . . ."

"You are *just* my sole heir," said Falk, speaking slowly. "My father is quite ill. After this war is

129

over, I will occupy his position—provided that I win, of course. And by the laws of our land, Elissa, you will inherit the throne from me. You are the future Queen of Castlemar."

Elissa's ears rang. She placed her palms against the sides of her face and pressed. Her cheeks felt hot.

Nana was right, she thought irrelevantly. *I do have cool hands.*

"Didn't you know?" he asked.

"No," whispered Elissa. "Bruno called you High Lord Falk. I thought you were a lord, like Bruno, only higher." Elissa didn't know what she was talking about. Her knowledge of the rankings of nobility was scanty at best.

"My father is the King," said Falk simply. "But only the court is required to address me as Prince Falk. In outlying areas they call me by the old title High Lord. By custom everyone else simply calls me Lord Falk."

Elissa wasn't listening. She was finally figuring out the true meaning of the phrase "bargaining chip."

"And you came for me because you wanted to trade me for troops," she said tonelessly.

130

Falk cleared his throat. "More of a loan, really," he said. "It wasn't meant to be permanent."

Elissa could feel her heart beating very slowly. She felt that if she moved even a fraction of an inch, it would stop. She concentrated on the steady *thump, thump, thump.* Somewhere in the distance Falk was speaking.

"Just a few months," he said.

Elissa squeezed her eyes shut. *Don't notice me,* she thought. But her old trick no longer worked. The pain had already found her. And from now on, no matter how silent and still she might keep, she would never feel safe again.

∽ 8 ∽

The Citadel of the Khan

Elissa had grown so pale that Falk stopped speaking. But there was one more thing he wanted to say.

"Elissa—" Falk began.

Before he could finish, the tent flap was flung aside, and in strode the old desert leader, accompanied by two younger men. The two young men were obviously brothers. One limped, and the other bore a bruise on his cheek. The looks they cast in Falk's direction were hostile. But when they noticed Elissa, their expressions changed to a mixture of respect and fear. They looked down immediately. One of the men murmured something to the old man, who cast a pointed glance at Elissa. His eyes darted back and forth, as though he was doing some very fast thinking. He made a short, dismissive gesture with his right hand to the two young men, who quickly departed; then he moved forward, both hands extended, palms up.

"I apologize for my inexcusable lack of hospitality," he said as he lowered himself gracefully onto a floor cushion.

He clapped his hands twice. At once the tent flap was pushed aside and a doe-eyed young boy entered, bearing a gleaming brass tray upon which were arranged several small glasses of greenish tea and a plate of dark fruits. The elderly man motioned for them each to take a glass and some fruit before serving himself. Then he positioned himself so that he sat facing Falk.

"Please partake of my pitiful fare," he proclaimed. "Eat! Drink!" He took a loud sip of his tea, inviting the others to do likewise. Mechanically, Elissa took the tea when it was offered her. It tasted strongly of mint and was shockingly sweet. Whether due to the sugar or the effect of the concentrated mint, Elissa began to feel revived. The numb feeling in her chest subsided. Her eyes began to focus.

"What brings you to my humble tent?" inquired the old man politely.

Falk hesitated for a second or two, but decided not to point out that their arrival had not been entirely voluntary. It was clear the old man was allowing him to open the conversation.

"We came to meet with the Khan," he began, hoping that a direct statement would put a close to the ritual nature of the conversation and lead to some concrete information. "Your master."

"Not so," contradicted the old man. "We are called the Blue People, but we call ourselves the Free People. Lords on earth there may be, but we have no master. None save Ankaa," he proclaimed, lifting his eyes and hands upward devoutly. Then he turned his head and smiled confidentially in Elissa's direction. "You do know that, don't you?" he murmured.

Not knowing what to say, Elissa nodded. This response seemed to satisfy the old man.

"But we will take you to him." He clapped his hands again. The two young men had evidently been waiting outside the tent, for they entered immediately.

"My sons will accompany you to the Citadel," he said. "After you have eaten and rested, you will depart. Your soldiers will wait here for your return." The three men then bowed and left the tent, leaving Falk to wonder what had just transpired. He also wondered what had become of Aldric.

Falk did not have long to ponder, for within a minute or two the young boy who had brought them their tea returned, bearing a platter laden with steaming bowls. He was followed by Aldric. The boy flashed a brilliant smile as he departed, but he kept his eyes carefully averted from Elissa's face.

"There you are!" exclaimed Falk. "Where on earth have you been?"

"I was just looking around," said Aldric. "Nobody seems to care where we go as long as we stay inside the camp. That curved knife you confiscated," he continued as he helped himself to a plate of spiced rice. "I've seen lots like it."

"I thought as much," said Falk. "I believe we may have already met the chief's two sons under less harmonious circumstances. These are definitely the men who attacked us. And now they are going to accompany us to meet the Khan." Falk frowned. "They are behaving very strangely."

"As long as we arrive in one piece," said Aldric cheerfully. He dug into his food. The knowledge that the mission wasn't lost, and that nobody was going to be killed, for now, had restored his appetite. "What is your plan?"

"I have been thinking," said Falk. He adopted the tone of a man who is about to make a concession and glanced at Elissa. She had not uttered a word since their conversation. She hadn't even raised her eyes. It was time for him to finish the thought that the old desert leader had interrupted.

"If we can manage to escape, I might be able to find some other way of financing this war. Perhaps the silk guild in Gravesport will make me a loan. But first we'll return Elissa to High Crossing, where she will be safe."

At the mention of High Crossing, something sparked to life in Elissa. Since her conversation with Falk, she had felt a curious detachment from everything around her, as if she were floating. Nothing really seemed to matter anymore. But going home—back to the valley, where no child other than old Nana's orphan was left alone; back to Nana, who had not even said goodbye;

and to the Manor, with Bruno's happy, bustling family, his adored children, his loving wife; being discarded because she wasn't useful any longer—that was unbearable.

"I am not returning to High Crossing." Elissa found herself speaking. "I am going to the Citadel." The two men looked at her in surprise.

"I have decided that I will go to the Citadel of the Khan."

"The girl speaks!" murmured Aldric. He glanced over to where Falk was gazing raptly at Elissa with the focused attention he normally reserved for newly acquired hawks.

"Do you understand what this arrangement entails?" Falk asked. "You must stay with the Khan until the war is over. Until his soldiers are returned, along with compensation for any who might be wounded or killed, you will have to remain in the Citadel."

Elissa nodded her agreement.

Falk clapped her on the shoulder. "You are truly my daughter," he said.

I hate you, thought Elissa.

Falk, Aldric, and Elissa set out on horseback for the Citadel of the Khan that evening, with Gertrude trailing reluctantly behind. Falk left the remainder of his soldiers at the forest's edge to wait for their return. There was no point bringing them. As the desert chief pointed out, food and water would be scarce on this journey. They were accompanied by the leader's two sons and two more tribesmen, who acted as guides rather than guards, for the desert itself made the perfect prison. As they traveled, the leader's sons lost their hostility toward Falk and Aldric. They even went so far as to treat them with grudging respect, though they still would not look directly at Elissa, their fear of djinns apparent in their downcast eyes. The huge expanse of inhospitable landscape that surrounded them on all sides encouraged a certain wary camaraderie.

After they set out, it only took a few hours before all recognizable landmarks had vanished, leaving just the monotonous, dusty surface of the desert topped by a vast sky. The day's travel was restricted to morning and evening, when the sun was at its weakest. They would rise before dawn and proceed until close to noon. Then they would stop, set up their tents, and share a meal, which mostly consisted of the sweet, dry fruits they'd eaten when they first arrived, and a pasty gruel. Afterward, everyone slept until close to sunset. Then they would load up the animals and travel by the light of the moon and stars until midnight. The brief alternating periods of sleep and travel had the effect of lengthening each day and distorting the hours, so the days seemed to slip by in a continuous unmarked stream.

There was little talk. The silence of the desert seemed to discourage interruption by human, or indeed any other, voice. Elissa welcomed the respite. She had no wish to speak to anyone. The knowledge that in her father's eyes she was merely a *means to an end*, a possession to be sold, traded, or discarded at whim, had hardened something within her, like a fist clamping around her heart. The desert—harsh, dry, and empty—reflected her mood.

I never had a father before, she thought. *I don't need one now.*

One by one she banished her hopes, her expectations, her illusions. She comforted herself with the idea that once she reached the Khan's

Citadel, her new life would begin. The Khan would treat her with the deference due a princess, and perhaps some genuine respect. They might even develop a friendship. This wasn't too far-fetched a proposition. After all, the Khan couldn't possibly be worse than her father. With luck she might be able to convince the Khan to let her stay, for she had no intention of going with her father to Castlemar.

The desert stretched on and on. At midday, when the sun had flattened every shrub, cactus, and boulder into a flat, dull sameness, Elissa could easily imagine the concept of infinity. But at midnight, when they made camp, the cover of darkness provided a canopy of intimacy for the travelers. The blue-robed tribesmen sat close to one another as they ate, chatting quietly, laughing over shared jokes. Falk and Aldric usually ate together, a little apart from the larger group, while Elissa took her supper in her tent.

"How is she?" asked Aldric one night.

"She seems well enough," said Falk. "Why do you ask?"

"She's awfully quiet. Did she take things badly when you spoke to her in the tent?"

"Quite the contrary," said Falk. "You saw her. She listened and she agreed."

"Yes. That was very convenient, my lord," said Aldric.

"I didn't force her, if that's what you're thinking," Falk said sharply. But then he softened. "You know, Aldric, when she was missing, I thought perhaps it was for the best. But when I explained the situation to her, she was so calm."

"Calm?"

"Yes, calm. She didn't make a scene, didn't shout or throw a fit. She didn't even cry, not a single tear."

"Did you expect something of that sort?"

"Why, yes," Falk admitted. "I did. I expected tears, at least. After all, she has been very sheltered. She knows nothing of the outside world. But when she didn't cry, I assumed—"

"You assume too much, my lord," said Aldric. "How many tears did you shed when your father threw your life away?"

"I wasted no time on tears," said Falk.

"Exactly," replied Aldric. "I wouldn't underestimate her if I were you. She is your daughter, after all."

Falk tented his hands before his mouth. "In that case, I should be very worried."

Aldric rose. "It's never too late to correct an error, my lord." He put a hand on Falk's shoulder. "But I wouldn't wait too long."

"How long is 'too long'?"

"You'll know when you've missed your chance," said Aldric. "I'm going to bed."

Falk watched him go. Aldric was probably right about Elissa. But he'd made his decision. It was too late to change it now.

For Elissa the days passed in a haze, seeming to prove that, like time, the desert has no end. Some things just go on forever, she thought. Sky, desert, loneliness. Do any of these things have limits? Even endurance has no limit. If it had, then there would be no people at all here, for one had to be as enduring as a rock in order to survive this place. And yet, after days of ringing silence, the solitude of lands uncluttered by human habitation, and the endless open sky, Elissa began to adjust to infinity. *In this place one can forget*, she thought.

And so Elissa was almost disappointed when she spied a line of small bumps on the horizon. They looked like large rocks. Another day and they became low hills. At midday a trick of the light made them shrink and flatten. Then, with the waning of the light toward evening, they popped back into three dimensions, turning into solid stone monoliths. It was only after another day had passed, however, that they were transformed into mountains of substantial size— overwhelmingly so once the party reached the base. There they stopped. The immense blocks of stone thrusting heavenward diminished all things—the travelers, the desert, even the sky. Elissa felt increasingly apprehensive as she gazed upward. She wondered if they would have to make an ascent. The climb would be arduous, if not impossible. She was certain that the only beings to have seen their lofty peaks were eagles.

That night they camped with the weighty mass of the mountain range at their backs, and well before dawn they set out along the base of the range, proceeding, as always, to the west.

Their shadows stretched long and thin before them, mimicking the deep crevasses of the stone giants. Elissa wished they would travel away from the mountains. Their massiveness made her feel increasingly small, as though she were shrinking. Still they advanced, until they neared the foot of a vertical wall that was so sheer, Elissa could not see a single hand- or foothold. The desert sun rose behind them, staining the cliff a deep, fiery red. Now she could see that what she had taken for the side of a mountain was an obstacle of an entirely different sort. Its smooth surface was a work not of Nature, but of human hands. Before them rose the massive walls of the Citadel of the Khan.

9

Sea Creature

No sooner had Falk's small party reached the gates of the Citadel than they were whisked inside by a waiting contingent of more blue-robed tribesmen. They dismounted and Elissa was immediately separated from the rest of the group by three women also clothed in deep blue. As she could not see their faces, she could only hope they meant her no harm. Reassuringly, they patted her arms and made comforting sounds as they led her through a mazelike series of tunnels and staircases. Halfway down a long hall they stopped at a latticed door, which they pushed open. Standing on either side of the door, they waited for Elissa to enter. Once they saw Elissa inside, the women quietly departed, leaving Elissa alone in a chamber unlike any she had seen before.

The room was spacious, and more ornately decorated than any chamber in Bruno's Manor. The floor was laid out in an intricate pattern of small tiles, forming a design so complex that Elissa became dizzy trying to follow it. The walls and ceiling were covered with tiles as well. In the middle of the chamber hung a gauzy curtain, behind which Elissa could just barely make out the contours of a large box. To Elissa, who had been raised in Nana's simple, unadorned cottage, the room was simultaneously beautiful and disturbing. It seemed excessive.

Elissa approached the veiled box with caution, wondering what it could be. She hoped it wasn't a coffin. The room exuded the timeless feel of a crypt. When she drew back the cloth, she was pleased to see a heap of exquisitely embroidered cushions. It was a bed! Her pack had been neatly placed on a chest at its foot, although Elissa could not imagine how it had gotten there. Could these be her own private quarters? Why, this single room was larger than Nana's whole cottage! After a week of sleeping on the hard floor of the desert, Elissa was tempted to curl up amid the soft cushions right then and there. She removed her cloak and outer garments and, once down to her shift, climbed into bed.

Before she could bury herself in the blankets, the door swung open and a young girl entered, bearing a shining copper tray upon her head and a pile of folded cloths in her arms. Elissa was relieved to see that she was not veiled. The girl winked merrily at Elissa as she kicked the door shut with the back of her heel.

The other women had remained silent, so Elissa decided to wait before asking any questions. They stood regarding one another. The girl was young, no more than nine, Elissa guessed. Her enormous liquid brown eyes matched the color of her hair, which she wore in two braids. In fact, she was the same even brown color all over—skin, hair, and eyes. And although she was a little plump, there was a kind of smooth sleekness to her. Elissa thought that the child looked very much like a seal. Instead of speaking, the girl shifted the cloths and, raising her arm, pointed to the wall. Elissa followed the line of her arm and found the outline of an arched door set in the tiles. The girl put the tray down and made an impatient gesture, which probably meant *Get up!* So

Elissa walked over to the opening, the girl following closely behind. Tentatively, Elissa pushed at the door. It swung open.

Much to her surprise, she found herself looking at a large pool of water. The room that surrounded it was gaily decorated with tiles, forming wave patterns. A fountain, entwined by a blossoming vine, tinkled musically at the other end of the room, spilling its bubbling contents into the pool. The sweetly perfumed air felt delightfully moist to Elissa's desert-parched nostrils. She wondered what exotic creature lived in this wonderful room. Elissa walked over to the edge of the pool and peered over the side. She saw nothing. She peered a little closer. Then, all at once, she was underwater. Elissa came up to the surface—furious.

"What did you do that for?" she sputtered.

"This is your bath," said the girl. "I'm supposed to help you get clean. But at the rate you were going, you would have taken all day."

Elissa hauled herself out of the water and sat at the side of the pool.

"You can speak!" she exclaimed.

"It sounds like you can talk too." The girl laughed.

Elissa quickly figured out that she was in the hands of a prankster and adopted a more direct form of communication. She reached out a hand and deftly shoved the girl into the water.

"There!" she said when the girl's shining head had broken the surface. "See how you like it!"

But the girl, instead of looking annoyed at the dunking, appeared delighted. Slipping easily out of her garments, she dove and somersaulted and slithered through the water with the natural ease of a sea creature. She behaved as though she had been born in the water. Elissa decided that her first impression had been correct. She succumbed to temptation and slipped back into the water herself. The two girls splashed and frolicked in the pool like two seals. When they emerged, sopping and happy, they were both thoroughly clean.

"Who are you?" asked Elissa as they patted themselves dry and donned robes.

"I am Maya," she said. "That means 'water.'"

Fancy that, thought Elissa. "My name is Elissa."

"I know," giggled Maya. "I'm your serving

girl. I am supposed to look after you until the wedding."

"Who is getting married?" asked Elissa.

Maya glanced at Elissa out of the corner of her eye, as if suspecting a trick. Then she leaned close and murmured in a low, almost conspiratorial whisper, "Aren't you the Khan's intended?"

"The Khan's intended *what*?" asked Elissa impatiently. It seemed to her that everybody else always knew what was going on ages before she did.

Maya shook her head and rolled her eyes expressively. "His bride," she said, sweeping her arm around the room.

Elissa could not believe what she was hearing. *Bride?* "That isn't possible," she said. "My father didn't say anything about marriage!" She looked into Maya's soft brown eyes. All at once she began to sob. The next thing she knew, she was spilling out her whole story to a transfixed Maya, who absorbed every detail with wide-eyed fascination.

"Maybe I am wrong," said Maya when Elissa had finished. "Your father sounds like a very important person. The Khan probably gave you the best chambers because your father is a prince."

"Perhaps," said Elissa without conviction. She didn't trust her father.

Maya patted Elissa, not understanding why she still looked upset. "In any case, the Khan can't marry you until you are fourteen, or until the moon has touched you. It's the law. You'll be back home before then."

"I'm almost fourteen!" cried Elissa.

Maya looked concerned. She gently laid her hand on Elissa's shoulder. "Has the moon touched you?" she asked.

Elissa shrugged, uncomprehending.

"Are you a woman?" asked Maya.

"No," said Elissa.

Maya smiled reassuringly. "Then you don't have anything to worry about." She paused for a moment. "You probably shouldn't tell anyone you're almost fourteen. The Khan might try something. He's very tricky. But your father probably knows that already."

Elissa had no idea what her father knew, or indeed how much her father had told the Khan.

However, she doubted he would have said more than he absolutely had to. Falk would never endanger his *own* position. Elissa sighed deeply.

"Don't worry," Maya said. "Just don't tell anybody anything. People gossip, and the Khan has lots of spies."

Elissa nodded. "That should be easy," she said. "Nobody here will speak to me."

Maya laughed. "The Blue women don't speak Common Tongue," she explained. "They only speak Tamayat. But I wouldn't say anything in front of them. They understand a lot more than they let on."

Then Maya, adopting the role of caretaker, wrapped Elissa up in the soft blankets and settled her in the bed. Ordering Elissa to *stay* as if she were a small puppy, she hung their wet clothes out on the balcony to dry, which, as she cheerfully explained, wouldn't take long at all. Finally she returned and crawled into bed next to Elissa, dragging along the copper tray, which much to Elissa's delight was piled high with sweets and delicacies. Elissa suddenly realized that she was starving.

"Let's eat," said Maya. "These are good." She

pushed over a small pile of flaky pastries that were stuffed with chopped nuts and dripping with honey. Elissa couldn't eat enough. The pastries were absolutely delicious! So were the tiny spiced bean-paste balls, which she consumed ravenously. There was a pile of soft, fragrantly steaming flat bread, which Maya showed her how to eat, tearing off a quarter at a time to dip into the dishes of sauces and pastes. They washed the meal down with a carafe of a sweet, slightly tangy fruit juice. Elissa, restored by the food, began to feel curious. It was the first time in many days that she had felt any interest in her surroundings.

"How is it that you have so much water here?" she asked. It had struck her as odd that in a desert they could afford the extravagance of a pool just for bathing.

"The Citadel is built on hot springs," Maya explained. "We use the water for bathing and for washing. The drinking water comes down from the mountain. And underneath the palace there is an underground lake. The lake is sacred. Except for the Khan, a few priests, and the Khan's mother—she knows everything—nobody even knows where it is. And if somebody happens to find out . . ." Maya drew a finger across her throat dramatically. She popped a grape into her mouth. "I'll take you to see it sometime."

"*You* know where it is?" Elissa was simultaneously thrilled and alarmed at the invitation. "How did you find out?"

"Oh, I have my ways," murmured the girl.

Elissa suspected that sleek little Maya had more "ways" than anybody would guess from looking at her. In a state of wonder and delight, Elissa watched Maya eat grapes. She'd never talked with such ease to another person before. The most wonderful thing was that Maya didn't seem to mind talking with her. In fact, she looked perfectly happy chattering away. Elissa wanted to know everything about her.

"Do you live here with your parents?" Elissa asked.

Maya looked down. "No, I'm alone," she said.

"Where are they?" Elissa wondered if they might be dead, in which case she and Maya would have something in common. Except that Elissa's father wasn't dead. She kept forgetting that fact.

"They are probably still home," replied Maya.

"Where is that?" asked Elissa, curious. Maya did not look like a mountain girl, or a Northern child. She was too dark.

"Oh," said Maya, "my home is in Suleskerry." She fell silent.

"Where is Suleskerry?" pressed Elissa.

"It's in the South Sea," she said, twirling the end of her hair around a finger. "It's an island." For the first time, Maya seemed reluctant to talk.

"I bet that's why you swim so well," said Elissa, encouraging Maya to speak.

"Oh, yes," Maya said. "I could swim before I could walk."

"I don't doubt that," said Elissa. "So how did you get here? The Citadel certainly isn't anywhere close to the sea."

"Well, we were with our Mother when a typhoon came up very quickly. Sometimes that happens. They come up so fast, you can't imagine. I got separated from the rest." Maya's face was scrunched up, as if she were trying hard to remember.

"Oh! Weren't you terrified? It must have been terrible to be lost at sea!"

"Well, no, not really. The waves look big and dangerous, but all you have to do is drift along."

Elissa gazed at her companion in wonder. "Drift along? During a typhoon?" The seal image floated before her eyes. Snuggling back in the pillows, Maya continued.

"After a while, maybe it was a day or two, a boat came along and picked me up. I had drifted a long way north. Since I was a child, they decided to sell me. So they took me to one of the port markets. I forget which one. The Khan keeps buyers all along the coast. One of them bought me and fetched me here. He was an awful man." Maya made a face. "Very ugly."

"They *sold* you?" Elissa was horrified. "How terrible!" She dropped her voice. "Was it the desert people who bought you?"

To Elissa's surprise, Maya laughed. "The Blue People? Heavens, no!" she exclaimed. "They'd sooner slit their own throats than buy somebody."

Then she regarded Elissa seriously. "I won't be here forever, you know," she said. "I will go home as soon as I can find a way back."

Elissa believed that Maya meant what she said. But no child, even one as clever as Maya, would be able to escape alone and unaided across the desert. She would need help. In spite of herself, Elissa couldn't help but think of Falk.

Elissa's hopes for her father had disappeared. She had no illusions about their relationship anymore. But if she was useful now, she might also be useful to him in the future. In that case he might indeed return for her, and perhaps when he did, he could find a way to free Maya.

I wouldn't be asking him to do anything for me, Elissa thought. *So I wouldn't owe him anything. After all, Maya's only a child.* Another question occurred to her.

"Why did the Khan want to buy you, anyway? It seems like he's got enough servants."

"The Khan never has enough servants," said Maya. "Or wives. He never has enough of anything."

"Oh," said Elissa, disappointed. From the way Maya described him, the Khan seemed both greedy and lazy. Even worse, he kept slaves, which was unforgivable. She wanted to know more, but she could not pursue the topic because Maya had fallen asleep. Made sleepy by her bath and her full stomach, Elissa soon drifted off herself.

She dreamt she was home, in Nana's cottage. It looked just as it had the last time she saw it, except that instead of Nana's round hearth, there was a round pool at the center of the room. Elissa walked toward the pool. The water was very dark and very still—like a mirror. She couldn't tell how deep it was, but she had the feeling, as she looked at its surface, that it went down forever. She recognized her own reflection in the water, but her face looked different somehow. Then, as she gazed, there was a ripple on the surface, and a seal's face broke through. It wiggled its whiskers at her and smiled. "I've found you!" Elissa cried joyously. Then Nana was beside her. In her hands she held a flint and a bellows. "You will need these," said Nana. "But be quick! Time is running out!" Someone was pounding on the cottage door. The pounding got louder and louder.

Elissa awoke to the sound of rapping on her bedroom door. She half sat up in bed.

Three women entered. As before, they were veiled, so Elissa couldn't tell if they were the same three who had brought her here. Their robes were loose enough to have hidden anybody inside them. One of the women was holding a shimmering garment in her hands. She said something, and when Elissa didn't answer, she repeated it.

Elissa shook Maya awake. The little girl stirred and rubbed her eyes. "What is it?" she said sleepily.

"Some people are here," said Elissa. "What do they want? I can't understand them."

Maya sat up in the bed and yawned. The woman said nothing more to her, but simply held out the silky garment, as if that were enough of an explanation. Apparently it was, for the little girl nodded, looking unusually grave.

"Well?" asked Elissa. The expression on Maya's face was making her nervous.

"It is time for you to meet the Khan," said Maya softly.

10

The Banquet

"How am I supposed to wear this?" wondered Elissa. She held the dress up against her with just the tips of her fingers, as if it were made of spiderwebs.

The cloth was beautiful. It was a very fine teal silk, marbled with pale leaf greens and aquas. But the gown, for all its volume, didn't seem to cover very much of her. It reached decently to her ankles, but the sleeves were slit so that her arms showed—every inch of them. Elissa's eyebrows were scrunched together in a combination of horror and intrigue. Elbows were never exposed in High Crossing.

"What's wrong with the sleeves?" she asked.

"It's what the palace women wear," explained Maya. "The slits keep you cool."

"*They* aren't wearing . . . this," Elissa said, pointing at the three dark-robed women.

"No," admitted Maya. "They're Blue People."

Handing her a pair of embroidered slippers, one of the women said something to Maya.

"They want you to put it all on," said Maya, placing the slippers at Elissa's feet. She helped Elissa into the gown, gathered the gossamer folds around her shoulders, and then stepped back to admire her.

"You look really beautiful," she said, smiling.

"Do you think so?" asked Elissa, trying to hold the fabric so that it covered her arms.

The women spoke to Maya. Maya shrugged and made a face.

"I can't come with you," she said.

"You have to," said Elissa. "I can't go alone."

"You won't be alone," said Maya. "There will be twenty-seven wives and a couple hundred concubines. Not to mention court officials."

As Elissa was led through the winding hallways that honeycombed the palace, she wished with all her heart that Maya were walking next to her. The three women swished around her, as silent as ghosts. And even if they *had* spoken,

Elissa wouldn't have been able to understand them. If only Maya were here, prattling away. She would calm the buzzing in Elissa's head: What should she say to the Khan? How was she supposed to behave? Was her father going to be there? Did she care? Elissa's nervousness increased as they approached the end of the corridor. She decided that the safest course of action would be to remain silent, just like the women who accompanied her.

The party came to a door, which, like all doors in the palace, was constructed of interwoven wooden slats. One of the women pushed gently, and the door opened to reveal a small chamber lined with rugs and cushions. On three sides the walls were hung with tapestries. The fourth was entirely composed of latticework. Elissa approached the intricate lattice. It was the first time she'd seen an entire woven wall. The complex star weave formed by the narrow interlocking bands of wood held her attention, but then as she focused beyond them, she realized that the wall was separating her from empty space. She was standing on a balcony. *This must be a good place to observe people in secret,* she thought. Observers could see out, but nobody could see in, and the rugs and tapestries would muffle any sounds the onlookers might make. She looked out upon the room below and saw that it was a large domed chamber. A circle of keyhole-shaped windows around the base of the dome allowed soft, milky light to drift down between dozens of gleaming white columns. The dome was painted to portray the night sky in summer. Elissa identified several constellations. *It looks so real,* she marveled. Then she dropped her gaze from the false heavens to peer through the slats. She would not have admitted this to anyone, but she was hoping to see a familiar figure dressed all in black.

As it happened, the room was completely empty of people, though it looked as though they were due to arrive at any moment. The entire center of the room was filled with trays of food, which had been spread out on intricately patterned rugs. In the midst of the trays an elaborate three-tiered fountain tinkled. Elissa wondered where the guests were meant to consume the food, as there were no tables or chairs to sit upon, just mounds of pillows heaped against the walls. Elissa's stomach grumbled at the thought of food. In spite of her afternoon feast with Maya, she felt hungry.

Elissa did not have to wonder long, for within moments the huge double doors at one end of the chamber opened, and people poured in. They were all youths, some quite young. Each boy was dressed in a pair of billowy white pants and a crimson vest. They entered quickly and quietly, taking their places against the walls. Elissa guessed that these were serving boys, probably slaves, given the Khan's penchant for buying his servants. Soon after they took their places, two guards entered, followed by perhaps two dozen women dressed in plain dark gowns cut very much like her own. The guards escorted the women to the back of the room, behind a low dais, and left once the women had settled themselves comfortably on mounds of cushions.

Those must be the Khan's wives, thought Elissa. Unfortunately, she could not get a look at their faces. If they were young or old, beautiful or plain, nobody could tell because they were all heavily veiled. She thought of Lady Hilde bustling about with her cheery smile, the efficiency with which she directed the household staff and managed the larder. And she remembered the pride shining in Bruno's eyes when he stood beside her at the summer fair. These shrouded women, sitting quietly, didn't even look like they were speaking to one another. *Some kind of marriage!* she thought. *Nobody sees you, nobody hears you. You might as well not exist.*

Then the guests arrived.

Elissa had never seen such finery. The whole room sparkled. The men wore hip-length orange tunics embroidered with gold beads and sequins. Beneath their bright tunics, striped bloomers extended to their calves. And on their feet they wore the strangest shoes Elissa had ever seen. The toes curled upward nearly to the knee. Elissa could see that these were not desert men. They wore mustaches that extended down along either side of their mouths, whereas the Blue men had all been clean-shaven. The women were also dressed extravagantly. Elissa recognized the dye technique of Castlemar weavers, for unlike other silks, these subtly shifted color and hue with every change of angle. Over their silken gowns they wore floor-length sleeveless tunics, which, like the men's, were encrusted with sequins and beads. Elissa guessed that these must be the Khan's concubines.

Most interesting of all for Elissa was the fact that, unlike the wives and the Blue women, the concubines wore no veils. Coiled around their necks and over their thick black hair were long strings of coins, which clinked and tinkled whenever they moved. Some of them had mysterious symbols painted on their foreheads and around their eyes. Elissa thought they were very beautiful. At the sound of a gong, everyone turned toward the massive double doors through which they had entered. Three small red-vested boys entered bearing yet more pillows and fans. They were followed by an old woman, who was dressed simply in a loose-fitting white robe. The guests remained dead silent as she walked across the hall and was settled amid the cushions beside the dais. It was curious that no one bowed to her, as it was clear just from her bearing that the old woman was a great personage. But Elissa noticed that the guests looked down in respect as she passed.

Soon a second entourage entered, this time with cymbals, horns, and drums. Apparently the Khan liked to make his entrance accompanied by a great deal of fanfare. Elissa peered intently through the lattice. Which one of these tall, imposing men could be the Khan? They all looked like men powerful enough to govern the Southern Kingdoms. As it turned out, he was not at all difficult to identify.

The Khan was monstrous. He was so huge that his litter was borne by six men. Perhaps he was so heavy that his feet could not bear his weight. Or perhaps he merely enjoyed being carried. Elissa could not determine which of these two reasons might serve to explain why a grown man would choose to be hauled about like a helpless child. Unlike the reception given the old woman in white, this time the crowd did not remain silent, but cheered loudly and bowed low as the Khan passed, although Elissa noticed that they did not smile. It took a troop of servants to settle the Khan into his cushions. When his attendants spread his peacock robes about him, he looked like he was swimming in a lake, with only his head appearing above the water. As Elissa gazed down at him, she thought that he resembled a giant floating pig.

The room appeared to be filled, yet there remained an expectant air among the guests. Elissa surmised that the guest of honor had not yet arrived. She guessed that it must be her father, for after the Khan had settled himself, a horn blew a single note and the crowd fell silent. Shortly afterward her father appeared in the doorway. In contrast to the Khan's gorgeously clad concubines and the guests, he looked almost drab in his simple black coat and breeches. Yet even in his unadorned garments Falk commanded the attention of the room. As he cut through the crowd to the waiting Khan, a hush fell, as it had for the old woman. Falk looked neither to the left nor to the right as he advanced, but kept his eyes fixed upon the Khan, who was smiling broadly. Falk smiled as well, although his eyes could have frozen fire.

"Welcome, welcome, esteemed guest!" cried the Khan, not rising but extending his great arms before him in a gesture of greeting. His robes billowed out to his sides like two sails. "Welcome to my miserable hovel! You honor us with your presence!" Coming out of the Khan's mouth, the ritual proclamation of humility sounded ridiculous.

Falk faced the Khan squarely, but he turned his head to the woman in white, nodding respectfully to her before he spoke. "It is our privilege to receive your hospitality," answered Falk in measured tones. His voice was quite low, but it carried. Elissa was amazed that she could hear him so clearly. It sounded as though he were speaking right in her ear. The dome must have been designed to amplify sounds.

"But where is your captain?" asked the Khan.

"He will be along shortly," said Falk. "There is no need to wait."

"Then do be seated," said the Khan, indicating a pile of cushions to his left, beside the woman in white. Elissa noticed there was still an empty spot immediately to the Khan's right. One more guest was expected; perhaps the Khan's advisor had yet to arrive. Other than the old woman in white, Elissa had seen no other royal personage.

Falk was casting his eyes about the room. He turned his head casually to the left and to the right, scanning the crowd. Then he lifted his eyes to the balcony where Elissa was hidden. It seemed to Elissa that he was looking straight at her. He smiled—a small, private smile.

The Khan clapped his hands once.

Elissa heard the sharp clap and, seconds later, felt her shoulders grasped by one of the women. They had remained so still that she had all but forgotten their presence. One of them held her shoulders, while another sprinkled a few drops of fragrant oil on her head. Then the third withdrew a milky white gardenia from within her voluminous sleeve and placed it carefully behind Elissa's left ear. They quickly led her back through the balcony door, along a short corridor, and down a staircase to the great open doors. There they stopped. Elissa hesitated. One of the women placed a hand on the small of her back and gently pushed her forward. It appeared that Elissa was meant to walk across the floor of the great hall alone.

In her soft embroidered slippers Elissa made no sound, yet all conversation stopped as she entered. She stood at the entrance, uncomfortably aware of the silence. In her revealing garb, and under the gaze of all these strangers, she felt completely exposed. Worst of all, she felt the weight of the Khan's eyes upon her. Although the room was warm, she felt chilled. Elissa looked at the two men who sat across the room. Her father was gazing at her steadily. The Khan looked wonderstruck. She looked into Falk's eyes and chose the lesser of the two evils.

As Elissa walked toward Falk, the Khan's face stretched into a grin, which, thankfully, Elissa did not see. If she had, the look in his eyes would have alarmed her. When Elissa reached the end of the dais where her father was sitting, the Khan, who was virtually speechless with delight, waved to her.

The Khan pointed to his right. "Come sit beside me!" Elissa would have preferred to sit next to her father. As much as she hated him, or thought she hated him, her father was at least familiar. He was certainly less odious than this gigantic human slug. She made her way to the Khan's side and sat on the cushions.

"Welcome to my abode, my pearl," he whispered to her. "I hope you will be very happy here."

Glancing at him out of the corner of her

eye—she wanted to avoid taking in the full effect of his face—Elissa replied that she was sure she would be.

The Khan clutched at his heart. "Your words are food for my starving soul."

Elissa very much doubted that. The Khan stared at her, transfixed, until the white-robed woman cleared her throat.

The Khan held his hands up, hushing the assembly. "Tonight we welcome our honored guests—Lord Falk, Prince of Castlemar, High Lord of the Eastern Reach, and his royal daughter, Elissa, who has deigned to grace my humble home with her beauty and charm." He gestured to Falk and Elissa, beaming. "Let the feast begin!" he cried. In unison, all the serving boys sprang into action. The guests settled themselves comfortably on the cushions, lying back while the boys ran between them bearing tray upon tray heaped with delights. The enticing aroma of the food made Elissa faint with hunger. Why was she so hungry? She had spent all afternoon eating. Maybe it was the dry desert air. In any case, she could not wait to be served.

Unfortunately, the Khan insisted on serving

her from his own plate, and with his own greasy fingers.

"You shall always have only the best, my jewel," he murmured as he passed her a ball of fragrant spiced rice. Elissa's stomach had its own demands, and little pride, so she ate almost everything he offered her, declining anything that looked like meat. There was plenty for her to eat, and it was all as delicious as the mouthwatering aromas had promised. There were mounds of herbed semolina and saffron rice, piles of okra lightly fried in golden batter, sizzling kabobs, and succulent stuffed mushrooms. Serving boys passed around platters of vegetables stewed in fragrant sauces. There were savory cheese pies with cinnamon-speckled crusts, and great stacks of lovely soft, flat breads with which to scoop up the seasoned pastes and spreads. Luscious fruits lay nestled in baskets that the boys carried upon their heads, as their hands were busy wiping the fingers of the guests with moist, perfumed towels. In the center of the room the fountain burbled with sweet wine, from which the guests continually filled and refilled their glasses. All the while, musicians played beautiful haunting melodies that sounded like women weeping. Dancers wove among the dining guests, gracefully twirling their wide skirts. Jugglers and acrobats leapt and performed wonderful tricks.

This certainly tops feast day in High Crossing, thought Elissa. *Cook would die of envy if she could see this.*

Elissa ate until she could eat no more. Then she eased herself back into the cushions with a small satisfied groan. At last she was full!

"Have you finished?" The voice was her father's. He was standing beside her. Elissa leaned forward and saw that Aldric had taken her father's place and was talking with the Khan. Aldric must have entered the room while she was busy with supper. Falk sat down, and Elissa sidled toward him, away from the Khan. Falk was smiling indulgently at her, his eyes crinkled in amusement. If she hadn't known better, she might have believed that he actually cared about her.

"Almost," she replied. "What's for dessert?"

Falk started to laugh in disbelief, but Elissa's words were prophetic. Serving boys entered, staggering under immense copper trays stacked high with delicate confections—coconut cakes, flaky pastries, honey puffs, candied rose petals and orange peels, fluffy nougat laced with gooey caramel sauce, stuffed dates, and snowy mint creams. Elissa eyed them. She had eaten so much, she was beginning to wonder if she could walk.

All at once Elissa remembered Gertrude. Here she had been stuffing herself and hadn't even given Gertrude a thought! Elissa's eyes filled with tears. She told herself that Gertrude was fine. Besides, Gertrude didn't even like sweets. Still, Elissa worried. What if they weren't taking good care of her? What if they weren't *feeding* her? Her father was looking at her curiously. Elissa regained her composure. What was wrong with her tonight? First she couldn't stop eating, and now she was getting all teary-eyed. Maybe she was contracting some illness.

"Are you all right?" asked Falk.

"Yes," said Elissa. Perhaps it was all the food, which was making her very sleepy, or perhaps it was the result of having shared confidences with Maya, but she had the sudden irrational desire to talk to Falk. She wanted to tell him how much she disliked the Khan, but she was sitting right next to him and didn't dare speak.

"My business with the Khan will be concluded tomorrow," said Falk. "Aldric and I will be leaving soon."

Elissa's heart sank.

"I will leave your . . . pet," said Falk.

"Pet?" For a moment Elissa had no idea what Falk was talking about. "Oh, yes. Gertrude." Gertrude would be a comfort.

"Don't worry, you will be well cared for," said Falk.

In spite of her distrust, Elissa wanted to believe Falk. Alone, she could never be a match for the Khan, and there was a limit to how much little Maya would be able to protect her.

Abandoning his conversation with Aldric, the Khan leaned back in Elissa's direction. Falk rose and resumed his place by the woman in white, who, it turned out, was the Khan's mother. Elissa wasn't sure how much more she could endure of the Khan's attentions. Moreover, with all that she had eaten, she felt desperately sleepy. Fortunately, the banquet was soon over. Before she knew it, she was once again whisked away by the Blue women. She made her way back to her chambers on legs that had turned to lead. When she saw her soft bed, she gave a little moan of relief. "Good night, world!" she mumbled, and was asleep before her head hit the pillow.

In his own chambers the Khan was not yet asleep. His mother, dressed as always in her white robes, had come to tuck him in—as he insisted she do every night. She was trying to reason with him.

"You can't marry her," she said.

"Why not?" he whined. "She's a princess! And besides, I don't have a single other green-eyed wife."

"Listen to me, Khoonbish," said his mother firmly.

"Mother, you *know* I hate it when you call me that." The Khan tried to stamp his foot, but he was lying down and only succeeded in kicking the covers.

"You can't marry her," she repeated, "even if she does have green eyes and eats like a horse, because she is not of age, and now everybody knows it."

"Who put that blasted flower behind her ear?" cried the Khan. "I will dismember her personally!"

"It doesn't matter who it was," replied his

177

mother wearily. "The point is that she has not yet been touched by the moon. According to tribal law, she is still a child! If you marry her before her time, you will be breaking the law."

"I don't care about the law!" raged the Khan.

"Yes, you do," said his mother sternly. "The tribes will rebel. This is one rule you simply cannot break. You have to wait—or win Castlemar some other way. Meanwhile, you have obligations to fulfill."

The Khan looked as if he cared not one bit for his obligations, or about any promises he might have made. He was hardly an honorable man; nor was he a patient one. "I can't wait," he said. "Her father might come back before she comes of age."

"Then you will have to return her," said his mother.

"I will never give her up," vowed the Khan. "I will have her, one way or another!"

Gathering up her white robes, his mother left the room, closing the door firmly behind her. Not for the first time did she wonder what kind of man she had brought into the world.

11

Touched by the Moon

When Maya entered Elissa's chamber the next morning with breakfast, she found her still in bed. Elissa drew the coverlet over her nose when she saw the tray. The smell of food turned her stomach.

"What's the matter?" asked Maya.

"I don't want anything to eat. I don't feel well."

"You don't look so good," observed Maya. The young girl reached over the tray to touch Elissa's forehead. "You don't feel hot, but your face is pale. Paler than usual," she added. There were dark circles under Elissa's eyes. She looked as if she hadn't slept a wink.

"My stomach hurts," Elissa groaned.

"That's from stuffing yourself last night. The

serving boys were impressed," retorted Maya cheer-fully, though even as she spoke, she felt a small twinge of worry. "You didn't eat any meat, did you? Meat spoils quickly."

"No," said Elissa. "I never do."

"Then it's not bad meat," said Maya. "Where does it hurt? High or low?"

"Low," replied Elissa. "And my back hurts too." Elissa thought Maya was probably right. She'd eaten an awful lot last night, and in all like-lihood her intestines were overfull. "Don't worry, I'll be all right. Just let me rest for a while."

But Maya was already worried. Low pain might mean food poisoning. With a brief assur-ance that she would soon be back, she ran off to fetch a medicinal tea. Maya was not gone long, but when she returned, it was clear that Elissa's condition had worsened. She was no longer lying down but sitting bolt upright in bed, her sheets wrapped around her like a mummy. The expres-sion on her face was one of sheer horror.

"What is it?" cried Maya, nearly dropping the tea in panic.

Elissa did not reply but simply drew back the

sheets. Maya bent over to take a look. There were drops of blood where she'd been lying.

"Oh!" cried Maya, clapping her hand over her mouth. "You've been wounded!" She leapt to her feet, casting her eyes about the room for an attacker. Then a thoughtful expression crossed her face. "It's your moon," she said finally.

"My what?" said Elissa, confused.

"You have been touched by the moon," repeated Maya.

"You mean, it's my monthly?"

Maya nodded. She patted Elissa's shoulder in a congratulatory way. "Today you are a woman," she announced.

Elissa felt relieved but also a little disappointed. In High Crossing Nana would have held a special ceremony to welcome her into womanhood.

"Don't look so sad," said Maya sympathetically. "It is a great day when a girl becomes a woman. On my island all the women gather together and make garlands of sweet frangipani flowers. They hang them all over." Maya held her hands up over her head, then wove them around her neck and waist. "Then, when she is completely covered in blossoms, they walk with her into the sea to present her to the water goddess. One by one the blossoms float away on the waves. When the girl comes out of the sea, she is a woman and they all welcome her."

"That sounds nice," said Elissa. Maya looked lost in thought, as she always did when she talked about her island home.

"Help me wash the sheets," Elissa said practically. Now that she knew what the blood was all about, she was no longer frightened. "And fetch me some rags."

Maya ran to fetch a washbasin and some rags. She also stopped to prepare another tea, one that would ease the cramping. When she returned, she got Elissa out of bed, stripped down the bedcovers, and made the bed with fresh sheets. Then she tucked her back into bed with a cup of hot tea.

"This will help," she said. Elissa sipped at the concoction. It tasted like chamomile combined with raspberry and a touch of ginger. A good combination for cramping. They must have an herbalist here. Later she would ask. Meanwhile, she just sat and contemplated her new status while Maya ran off to wash the sheets before the stains set.

"Won't people be suspicious if I spend the day in bed?" asked Elissa when Maya returned.

"No," said Maya. "We will tell them that you ate too much. Everyone will believe that!"

Elissa now understood the reason for her insatiable hunger and for the teariness of the previous night. She sighed. Maya sighed with her.

"We will have a secret ceremony all of our own," Maya promised. "I will take you to the Sacred Lake, and the water goddess will receive you. We will go in a few days, when your moon has waned. Would you like that?"

Elissa smiled. She would like that very much.

"What do they do in your land?" asked Maya. "How do they present you to your goddess?"

Elissa thought of how to explain the practical, workaday life of High Crossing. "No goddesses, no gods," she said. "The family makes a party, and everybody sings and dances."

"And the new woman? What do they do for her?"

"Well," said Elissa, "she wears a special white dress, which her mother makes just for the occasion." Elissa stretched out her hands to indicate a long skirt and narrow sleeves. "Her father gives

183

her a gift, something nice for a woman, like a hair comb. Then she receives secret knowledge from the midwife, and the midwife gives her a talisman." Elissa was already aware of this knowledge, though it was supposed to be kept from young girls. In fact, most of the valley girls knew the "secret" long before their monthlies. After all, anybody could see how farm animals got their babies. Still, the talk with the midwife was special.

"What is the talisman for?" asked Maya.

Elissa wasn't sure how much to explain to Maya. The talisman was supposed to ease the pain of childbirth. "It's for protection," she said. "It's so she and her children will have good luck. And when there is trouble, it brings her comfort and strength. She is supposed to keep it her whole life. It's very special." Elissa was afraid she might start crying. Home was so far away.

Maya saw the tears in Elissa's eyes and flung her arms around her. "I will get you something special!" she cried. "Wait here." Elissa had no desire to go anywhere, so waiting was easy. Even though the tea had helped, she didn't feel at all like getting up. She began to feel sleepy and soon drifted off.

Maya left Elissa in great haste and headed straight for the guest quarters. As a mere child she was routinely ignored by everyone in the Citadel. What damage could a child do? Children were completely harmless. Adults nearly always miscalculated when it came to children. And it was that miscalculation that had allowed her to gain access to every nook and cranny of the great fortress. As she wound her way along the passages on the far side of the Citadel, where the guests were quartered, she thought of Elissa's sad face. Maya would bring her a wonderful present, one that would lift her lonely friend out of her misery.

Maya stopped in front of the short passageway to the men's guest quarters. Which door opened to Falk's chambers? There were several doors, but fortunately only two guests. Then she heard faint murmuring. She stood by each door until she could make out voices. The voices carried right through the door slats, for the doors were designed, like everything else in the Citadel, for eavesdropping.

Maya pressed her ear to the door and listened. One voice was asking something about arrangements being made for Elissa. The other said something about perhaps not winning a war. Then the first voice replied that he would return. Listening to that voice, Maya smiled. She knew she was in the right place, and that she had made the right decision. Maya lifted her hand to the door and rapped once, twice. There was a shuffling sound, and a moment later the door opened.

"Come with me," she said.

Elissa thought she had dozed off for just a few moments. But perhaps it was longer, for she awoke with a start to feel a hand on her shoulder. One of the Blue women was sitting next to her on the bed. Startled, Elissa struggled to sit up. The woman's hand stopped her.

"Don't get up," whispered the tribeswoman, pushing her gently against the cushions. Then with the other hand she pulled down the veil. It was her father! Elissa cried out in surprise. In spite of herself she was pleased.

"How did you—?"

"The child brought me," he said. "She told me you were sick and brought me these robes. This wing of the palace is strictly off-limits to men." He looked around her room, as if searching for secret listening holes. Spotting nothing suspicious, he relaxed. Leaning forward slightly, he studied her face.

"Are you very ill?" he asked.

Elissa hesitated for a moment. Normally a father would be proud to hear the good news that his daughter had become a woman. Unfortunately, Falk wasn't like other fathers. Elissa wasn't sure she could face another disappointment. She decided that the less she said to him, the better.

"No," she said quietly. "Not very. I just ate too much last night."

Falk nodded. "You certainly did." He paused.

"Elissa," he began, "the Khan has agreed to lend me his palace troops. They are great warriors, every one of them. I know the dispute will be resolved in a matter of months. Then I will return for you. I have the Khan's word that you will be well treated here. And Aldric has seen to it that I will hear of it if you aren't. He has made

187

certain arrangements. I do not doubt that the Khan will offer you every kindness." He hesitated. "But you must never be alone with him. Do you understand?"

Elissa nodded, remembering the way the Khan had looked at her. She felt a chill. If anyone found out . . .

"Are you sure you're all right?" asked Falk.

"I am fine," said Elissa quickly. "When will you go?"

"We are leaving this morning," he said. "I will come back for you very soon. I promise."

Elissa looked past him. *You won't come for me,* she thought. *You didn't before.*

"Elissa—" he began. The words were on his tongue, ready to be spoken.

He hesitated, then, unexpectedly, reached out and touched her cheek. "You look so much like your mother."

The breath caught in Elissa's throat. There were two sharp raps at the door—Maya's warning.

Falk rose to his feet. "No one will harm you," he promised. Then he was gone.

❧ 12 ❧

The Sacred Lake

Elissa remained in her room, waiting for her monthly to abate. The truth was that she felt fine after the first day, but Maya would not let her out of her chambers.

"I told everybody you were tired from your journey and wanted to rest, so they would leave you alone," said Maya. "We mustn't let anybody find out."

"What about next month?" asked Elissa. "You won't be able to tell them I'm tired from traveling."

"Don't worry," said Maya confidently. "I'll make up some other excuse."

Maya was insistent about washing Elissa's rags and bedclothes herself. She explained that she knew a secret washing place, where none of

189

the others could see her. Elissa suspected that little Maya knew a lot of secret places. She probably knew a lot about the Citadel too. Elissa took the opportunity of her "illness" to probe Maya.

"Why does the Khan have so many wives?" asked Elissa. The group of darkly garbed women at the banquet had stuck in Elissa's mind. "Aren't there enough servants to run the Citadel? And what about all those concubines? What does he do with them all?"

Maya laughed. She had just been for a swim in the pool and was stretched comfortably across Elissa's feet. "The wives don't run anything. He married them to make alliances with other kingdoms. And the concubines are just for show— like jewelry, or fancy clothes. When there isn't a banquet or official ceremony, nobody even sees them."

Elissa thought for a moment. "Is that why the Blue People serve him?" she asked. "Did he marry a Blue woman?"

Maya sat up, shaking her head emphatically. "No, the Blue People hate him. They'd never let one of their women marry him. It was the Khan's great-grandfather who married a Blue woman.

He stole her from the tribe. So now they are pledged."

"That must be why they hate him," said Elissa.

"They hate him for a lot of reasons," said Maya. "He stole the Citadel from them too."

"You mean the Khan didn't build it?"

"Oh, no. The Citadel is very, very old. Can't you feel it?" Maya rolled off the bed and put her hand on the floor. She nodded to Elissa, encouraging her to do the same. Elissa reached down and touched the tiles. They felt cool, nothing more.

Maya hopped back onto the bed, continuing her tale. "When the Khan's great-grandfather rode down from the steppes with all his horsemen"— she gestured vaguely in the air with her left hand—"they found the Citadel and they took it."

Elissa frowned in puzzlement. With its high walls, the Citadel didn't look very easy to "take." "How did they do that?"

"Well," said Maya, "they snuck inside somehow, and they killed everybody who lived here."

"Everybody?" Elissa was horrified. "Even the women and the children?"

Maya nodded briskly.

"No wonder the Blue People hate him!"

Maya shook her head. "The Khan's great-grandfather didn't kill any Blue People," explained Maya. "But this was a sacred place for the Blue People. And the people who lived here were sacred too."

"Who were they?" Elissa was intrigued. The concept of a sacred person didn't exist in Elissa's mind.

"They were the Ankaa," said Maya.

Elissa looked at her blankly.

"They were healers."

After a few days Elissa decided to bathe. In fact, Maya pushed her into the pool and made her wash very thoroughly. The little girl seemed very excited about something.

"Why are you hopping around like that?" asked Elissa.

"I am going to show you the Sacred Lake." Maya was flushed. "Look! I have brought your initiation robe." Maya held a length of white silk in her arms. She held it up for Elissa. The gown was simple but elegant. Tears came to Elissa's eyes.

"I made it myself," said Maya shyly.

Elissa was impressed. "Where did you get the cloth?"

When Maya laughed, it sounded like a cascade of bubbling water. "The Khan's sheets," she giggled. "I took one of them off the line. Don't worry, they'll never notice. He has hundreds of them."

"Well, I can see you are very talented with a needle," Elissa said. "It's lovely. Are we going soon?" Elissa was thrilled. She hadn't seen any part of the Citadel besides her own chambers and the banquet hall.

"I will come for you tonight at midnight. Everybody will be asleep, so no one will see us."

"Can you find your way in the dark?" asked Elissa.

Maya held her finger against the side of her nose. "Of course," she said, winking. "I have many talents," she added. Then she left to attend to her chores.

Elissa passed the day in a state of nerves. She would have loved to take a walk, perhaps in the gardens. She imagined there *must* be gardens somewhere. But she wasn't permitted to wander the palace unaccompanied, so Elissa paced her chamber impatiently. What if they were caught? Was the penalty really death? Elissa was so excited, it was difficult for her to fall asleep. Somehow she managed to doze off, only to be awakened by Maya's hand shaking her by the shoulder.

"Let's go!" said Maya.

Quickly, Elissa donned the white robe Maya had made for her.

"Slip this on," commanded Maya, handing her a black outer robe with a hood. "And don't make a sound!" Maya was already dressed in black. She carried a small black bag with her as well. Then, putting her finger to her lips, she opened the door, and they both slipped silently into the hallway. Small torches smoldering in brackets along the walls shed enough light for them to make their way, but just barely. Apparently nobody was expected to be up and about at this hour of the night. They followed the twists and turns of the hallway until they came to a door Elissa recognized. They had arrived at the balcony above the banquet hall. Maya pushed the door open and promptly disappeared.

"Where are you?" whispered Elissa. "I can't see a thing."

"I'm right here!" Maya whispered back. As Elissa looked in the direction of Maya's voice, she thought she detected a movement near one of the tapestries. Maya was behind it. The little girl extended a hand and pulled Elissa to her. The tapestry hid a narrow door, which Maya pushed open. Bending over, she dragged Elissa behind her. Then she shut the door.

The darkness was total. Elissa stood still, trying to locate Maya by sound. The silence was almost as deep as the darkness. From somewhere to her right came a small noise. Then a light sprang up.

"I brought a lamp," said Maya. Sure enough, she was holding a small oil lamp in her hand. "Nobody will see or hear us in here." Elissa could barely see anything herself—even with the light.

As they walked down the narrow passage, Maya told Elissa about the Citadel. Apparently it was filled with secret passageways. This passageway, she explained, led from the women's chambers to the balcony above the banquet hall, which was also used as an audience room, so that the Khan's mother could come anytime she liked in order to eavesdrop on the Khan's political affairs.

The balcony had formerly been intended for the Khan's ministers, in order to keep them up to date on the lies the Khan had told his enemies. The Khan's lies were so hard to keep track of, he needed all the help he could get. However, the Khan's unfortunate temper had cost him all of his ministers, which meant the balcony was no longer in constant use. Chances were good they would not run into anybody in the passageway, especially not at this late hour.

"Why does his mother want to listen?" asked Elissa.

Maya looked at her. "She can't control him anymore," she said finally. "There's been a lot of whispering lately. I think she may be planning something."

"What?" asked Elissa. But Maya didn't answer.

"We are coming to the end," Maya whispered.

It was indeed the end. They had come face to face with a rough rock wall. "What now?" Elissa whispered.

Maya was silent. She faced the wall, frowning as if in thought. Then she ran her fingers against the bottom until she found a loose chunk of rock. This she removed. Something gleamed in the hole. It was a lock! Maya withdrew a small key from her bag and placed it in the lock. A heavy stone door in the wall swung silently back. Then, carefully replacing the rock, she motioned Elissa through, quickly pulling the door shut behind them with an iron ring set into the stone. The door clicked into place.

Now they were in a passage that was very ancient indeed. Elissa could smell the years, taste the dampness of ancient earth. Maya's lamp bobbed faintly before her, descending gently with the downward slope of the floor. They walked in hushed silence, as though sensing the increasing weight of the earth above them. At one point Elissa reached out her hand to touch the walls. They were cool and moist. This was a place that had never felt the warmth of the sun. The passageway twisted and turned, and at times even seemed to double back upon itself. Elissa was growing very tired and was about to ask Maya if they could rest for a bit, when abruptly Maya stopped. Elissa was so sleepy that she nearly crashed into her. They had come to a dead end.

Maybe Maya had taken a wrong turn. They were lost! Elissa started to panic at the thought of being trapped forever in the bowels of the earth. She was tempted to run, anywhere, but there was no place to go. Was it her imagination, or was the tunnel shrinking inward? Maya must have sensed her fear, for she reached out and held Elissa's hand very tightly. As Elissa calmed herself, she realized why Maya had stopped. There was a subtle movement to the air. Maya leaned over and, scrabbling at the base of the wall, found what she was looking for—a tunnel. Maya crawled into it on all fours. Elissa bent over and peered into the gloom. "Please tell me there is another entrance," she said.

"There is," said Maya, her voice muffled. "But it's guarded. Just hold on to my foot."

Elissa crouched down and followed Maya, bumping into her from time to time as they crept along the damp floor of the tunnel on all fours. This was awful—far, far worse than the narrow passageway! Elissa tried not to think, but merely counted her breaths until they finally emerged through a rough hole. She stayed still for a moment and then raised her hand over her head, expecting a ceiling. The space above her was wonderfully empty. She straightened, and the two girls stood side by side in the small pool of light cast by Maya's lamp.

"Watch this," said Maya. She smothered the flame. Instead of being thrown into instant blindness, Elissa found that she could see. They were in an enormous cavern, the interior of which was bathed in a soft pink light. She looked about her in wonder. The cavern looked so much like a fairy castle, Elissa had to rub her eyes to make sure she was not imagining things. From the ceiling hung tier upon tier of delicate stalactites. Some were immense, reaching nearly halfway to the floor from the high peak, while others, tiny and sharp as cat's teeth, clung in countless rows among them. They glowed. The effect was breathtaking.

"You can breathe," said Maya, smiling. "They won't fall down. Come."

Elissa followed Maya to the middle of the great chamber, and there she saw the origin of the pink light. It was a lake. From what she could see, it was a large one—and it was glowing as if a light were submerged deep under its still surface. The far end of the lake faded into darkness. At first Elissa thought the glow simply stopped at the other shore, but on closer inspection she could see that the lake ended abruptly at a dark wall. In fact, it looked as if the whole wall had been charred by some ancient conflagration. *It must have been an enormous fire,* thought Elissa. Though how flames burned in a lake was beyond her understanding. Elissa looked into the water. From its depths the light glowed and shimmered. As she watched, it seemed to move in patches.

"What is that?" asked Elissa, pointing at one of the patches.

"Those are the creatures of the goddess," said Maya. "They're very small. Can you see?"

Yes, Elissa could see. The little creatures were making small darting movements in an intricate pattern. Elissa laughed in delight. They were dancing! She knelt and leaned closer. They moved to and fro, weaving in and out in a continual pulsing spiral, coming together, moving apart. The effect was hypnotic. Elissa gazed, transfixed, and discovered that she could hear them as well—a soft humming, rhythmic sound. It was like a song. If she concentrated, she could almost make out words. A small movement at her side broke the spell.

Maya was staring intently at Elissa. "The goddess speaks through them," she whispered. "Are they calling to you?"

"I don't know," whispered Elissa. "I hear something."

"It's time," said Maya. "The goddess wants you to come."

Maya lifted Elissa up by her hands and removed her black outer robe.

"I am sorry I don't have any flowers for you to wear," said Maya, standing back. Then Maya stripped off her own garments. Grasping Elissa by the hand, she led her into the water, singing in a sweet, high voice. Elissa did not understand the words, but somehow she grasped the meaning. The song was the sound of water itself. Soothing, rhythmic, flowing. The water swirled about her until Maya, with a final ululating trill, pushed her under. Once underwater, she could distinctly hear the words of the song. *Elissa,* sang the creatures. *Elissssa. Ellliiisssaaaa.* So high, so sweet. She never wanted to come back up to the surface. She wanted to stay with them forever, and would have if Maya had not hauled her out. She led her back to the shore, where they stood dripping. Then Maya gave Elissa a hug and kissed her formally, first on both cheeks and then on her forehead.

"Welcome," she proclaimed. "You are now a woman."

Feeling a little dizzy, Elissa sat down.

"I think the water goddess likes you," Maya observed. "Her creatures seem to like you too." She looked at Elissa, who was glowing.

Elissa felt wonderfully warm and contented, full.

"Open your mouth," said Maya. The inside of Elissa's mouth glowed bright pink.

"You must have swallowed some of the water," she said. "It will fade after a while. We need to get back now."

"Of course," said Elissa. She was not at all worried about the return through the dark tunnel. The truth was, she felt quite happy. She put her hand against the ground to lever herself up and felt something sharp beneath her palm. Without thinking, she picked it up and closed her fingers around it.

By the time the girls returned to Elissa's chambers, they were both bone tired. Maya helped Elissa slip out of her dress, which was no longer white but pink. Elissa crept gratefully between her sheets. She was so sleepy, she wasn't even aware that she still held the small object in her hand.

"How ever did you find that lake?" she mumbled as she dropped into slumber.

"I sniffed it out," said Maya. "Now go to sleep."

Maya slipped out into the hall and made her way back to her own room. She was so intent on getting back before dawn, she did not notice the black-robed shadow silently following her.

～ 13 ～

Om Chai

Elissa was awakened the following morning by the clatter of blinds being lowered against the fierce noonday sun.

"Wrmph?" she said. She cracked one eye open and was instantly blinded. "Aarnngh!"

"That's right," said Maya, unrolling the last of the blinds. "Time to get up."

Elissa yawned and came slowly awake.

"What time is it?" Her face bore the inward expression of someone who is trying to recapture an elusive dream.

"Lunchtime." Maya placed a tray on a small bedside table. The enticing aroma of bean patties and fresh bread filled the room. Maya expertly split one of the flat, round loaves and filled it while Elissa sat up and groggily arranged herself.

"How do you feel?" asked Maya, tearing off a chunk of bread with her teeth.

"I had the strangest dream last night," Elissa mumbled. "There was a dark tunnel and pink icicles, and you were there. . . ." She stopped speaking when she realized that she was clutching something. As she opened her hand, the previous night came back to her in a rush. It had not been a dream!

"What's that?" asked Maya.

"I don't know. I found it last night." Elissa shook her head, trying to force herself to come fully awake. She held the object up for Maya to see. It was a curved shard. On the concave side it was completely smooth. The convex side was etched with odd markings. Curious, Elissa held the shard up, turning it to study the pattern.

"Maybe the goddess gave you a talisman," suggested Maya.

Elissa was lost in thought. The shard was clearly a piece of a larger object. There was a squiggly line running through the center and jagged, roughly parallel lines around the edges.

Maya waved a pastry at Elissa. "These are good. I swiped them off the Khan's lunch plate just for you. Try one." She pushed a flaky morsel close to Elissa's hand.

"These markings don't look random," Elissa said. She was gazing at the shard in her hand, fascinated. If she tipped it at a certain angle against the light, she could almost decipher something.

"Are you going to eat that?" asked Maya.

"Of course not. It's made of clay, or stone or something."

Maya removed the object from Elissa's hand, shoving the pastry into its place. "Eat now!" she commanded. "You are delirious."

Elissa replied that she didn't feel particularly delirious, just a little preoccupied. However, after she had eaten, her head cleared and her strength returned. Smiling, Elissa stretched her arms over her head. She felt better than she had in weeks! Elissa held out her hand, and Maya returned the shard.

"Who would know about these markings?" she asked Maya.

Maya hesitated. "A gift from the goddess is very important," she said seriously.

Elissa waited for Maya to continue. "But what?" she finally asked.

"Umm, we'll have to leave the palace if you want to know what the gift means."

"You mean we'll have to go into the desert?" Elissa wondered how they would get through the huge gates of the Citadel.

"No," said Maya. "We'll have to go into the city. The Citadel is a *city*. The Khan's palace is only a part of it. Didn't you know that?"

Elissa shook her head. "I don't know anything." Maya was still silent. "What is the problem?" asked Elissa.

"They told me that if I let you go into the city, I'd get my head chopped off." Maya looked concerned, much more so than when she had suggested going to the Sacred Lake.

"Then let's not go," said Elissa. "We were lucky enough nobody caught us going to the lake."

But Maya wasn't listening; she had already made one of her quicksilver decisions.

"I'll be back soon. Get ready to go." She dashed out the door.

Elissa felt a little exasperated. Maya was usually more forthcoming. Nevertheless, she rose from her bed, washed her face and hands, and donned a light robe. The last few days had been very confusing. Elissa had so much to think about, so much to piece together. She felt bewildered, but when she looked at the shard in her hand, Elissa knew that she was on the verge of understanding something important. She opened her chest and rummaged around until she found the little velvet purse Nana had given her. She dropped the shard inside, then regarded the little purse for a moment, holding it lightly in her hand. It reminded her of home—of Nana and Gertrude. It seemed like ages since she had talked to Gertrude. Elissa frowned thoughtfully, then cut part of her bootlace to hang the purse around her neck. She wasn't about to let the shard out of her reach, not even for a moment.

The door opened with a soft whoosh.

"Here, put these on," said Maya, shoving a veil and hooded black robe into Elissa's hands. They were much like the ones they'd worn to the Sacred Lake. She spoke rapidly as Elissa slipped on the robe and adjusted her veil. "If anyone sees us, they'll think we're servants. We don't have much time. For the next two hours everybody will be taking the midday nap. If we hurry, we'll be back before anyone notices we're gone." Maya held her finger to her lips as she peeked out the door. The coast was clear.

"Where are we going?" whispered Elissa as they slipped silently into the hall.

"Just follow me. Quietly."

Elissa practically had to run to keep up with Maya. They flitted through the maze of halls like bats, turning first down one dark passage, then another. Elissa had no idea where they were headed, until, without warning, she was blinded by the brilliant light of day. As her eyes adjusted to the light, Elissa realized she was in a narrow courtyard. No, it was a street. She was outside! The thought made Elissa's heart leap. Oh, to be in the open air again! She missed the sound of wind in the trees, birdsong—the sky!

"This is the sewage collector's entrance," said Maya. "The guards usually don't watch it." She grabbed Elissa's hand, and soon the two girls were running like the wind down the narrow alley and into the city.

Only when the palace walls were out of sight did Maya slow to a walk. Elissa tried to catch her breath.

"Where are we going?" she panted.

"To see the Tea Maker, Om Chai." Elissa couldn't see Maya's face through the veil, but she could tell from the tone of respect in her voice that Om Chai must be a great person.

"Om Chai knows everything," said Maya. Then she put her finger to her lips. "Best not to talk."

Elissa nodded. Maya's head was at stake. As they walked silently along, she hoped Om Chai did know everything. There were so many questions she wanted to ask—starting with the shard. In the back of her mind, though, she had the idea that if Om Chai could read the markings on the shard, perhaps she could also tell Elissa what to do about her father—not that those two things were connected. She just needed to talk to someone who was knowledgeable in the ways of the world. Someone wise.

The two girls made their way through the streets at a comfortable pace. Elissa was disappointed that there was so little to see. Everywhere she looked, she saw nothing but bare white walls. Oddly enough, they did not run straight up and down but curved gently outward to meet the street. It was as though they had been poured or molded. *If Cook decided to make a city out of bread dough, this is what it would look like,* she thought. There were no sharp angles anywhere. No angles at all. Every surface was rounded, smooth, gleaming white. And the streets were completely deserted. There was not a soul to be seen. Elissa's eyes swept upward. She thought she would see a patch of blue, but the sky was hidden by overlapping lengths of soft gauze. Elissa grasped the purpose of the canopy, for even with the sun blocked by the cloth, the heat was oppressive. She groaned in frustration as they made their hushed way through the meandering white tunnels. Being outside was almost the same as being inside.

Maya grabbed Elissa's arm, forcing her to a halt. They were standing before a narrow blue door, which, as far as Elissa could tell, looked no different from all the other doors on the street. Maya pushed it open.

"Shouldn't we knock first?"

Maya raised her hand to quiet Elissa and nudged her through the doorway.

As she pushed the door shut behind them, Maya heaved a sigh of relief. "We're here."

The girls removed their veils and drew back their hoods, while Elissa wondered exactly where *here* was. The house, if this was a house, was so filled with smoke, she could hardly see. But she could smell, and what came to her nostrils was pure High Crossing. Rosemary, thyme, lavender, fennel, and mint wafted through the air. As her eyes adjusted to the dim light, Elissa made out the contours of a room, the ceiling of which was entirely covered by hanging bunches of herbs. The center of the room was occupied by a round hearth. A three-legged stool leaned against its edge. Elissa closed her eyes, half expecting to see Nana.

"Welcome, welcome." A bony hand touched Elissa delicately on the arm.

Elissa jumped in surprise. At first she thought a sparrow had landed on her arm. Then a small woman materialized by Elissa's side, seemingly out of thin air. Her small bright eyes flashed at Elissa, and her head tilted this way and that. Elissa expected her to chirp.

"Om Chai," said Maya, "I have brought a friend."

"I'm Elissa," she said.

"Yes, you are," the old woman said in a feathery voice. She took Elissa by the hand, leading her into the room. "Not to fear. Not to fear."

Maya followed along behind them as the ancient woman led Elissa to a low stool.

Om Chai winked. "Tea?" she asked. The girls nodded. As she poured the steaming liquid into two small cups, Maya explained the reason for their visit.

"A talisman," Om Chai whispered. "Give it to me."

Elissa drew the little purse out from under her robe and removed the shard. It felt warm to the touch.

"Ahhh . . ." Om Chai let out a long sigh and then sat silently as she held the small piece of baked clay in her lap. She sat so motionless that Elissa wondered if she had fallen asleep. With all the smoke drifting across the room, it became increasingly difficult to see her. Om Chai's edges seemed to blur and fade in the gloom. Elissa sniffed at her tea. It smelled of mint—only mint. She took a cautious sip.

"A piece of earth," said Om Chai. "Do not lose." She handed the shard back to Elissa.

Was that all? Elissa already knew that clay came from the earth. What about the markings? She was about to ask when Om Chai spoke again.

"You know Phoenix," she said. It sounded more like a statement than a question. Om Chai was staring at Elissa with an odd intensity. Her gaze did not waver.

Elissa nodded her head, hoping that Om Chai would not launch into the tale. If Nana had told her the story of the Phoenix once, she'd told it a hundred times. Elissa could practically recite it by heart: The ancient bird burned itself up so that it could rise in glory and begin life anew. It was somehow connected to the ebb and flow of the seasons. Elissa had not taken the story seriously. No bird would ever fling itself into a pit of flames. Om Chai was still looking at Elissa, obviously expecting her to say something.

"The Phoenix is a myth," Elissa said. It was the best answer she could give.

"Myth? That is very good." Om Chai unexpectedly let out a wheezy laugh, though Elissa could not see anything funny about what she had just said. All the old tales were myths, weren't they?

"Myth tells you *who you are*," said Om Chai.

She lifted a finger and pointed at Elissa's head. "You do not know who you are, but Phoenix knows."

Then, as Elissa had predicted, Om Chai settled back and began the tale. "Mark my words! Phoenix must fling herself into her fire *every thousand years,* or the earth will dry up like an autumn leaf and the world will end. When her time comes, Phoenix will cast Seeker into the world. Seeker will gather five elements, Earth, Wind, Fire, Water, and Spirit"—Om Chai jabbed her finger in the air with each element—"and bring them to Phoenix. Then Phoenix will be reborn!"

This was a different version of the story. Elissa had not heard of the Seeker before, although she was familiar with the five elements.

Om Chai had stopped speaking. It looked like she was about to drift off. Elissa did not want to sit there waiting, so she spoke up.

"What does this mean?" she asked, holding out the shard and pointing at the lines.

Om Chai cocked her head and smiled. *"Here you come,"* she said. *"There you go."*

This is one wise woman who makes no sense at all, thought Elissa. But those lines had to mean

215

something. Before Elissa could ask again, Om Chai began to chant in a whispery singsong. "Phoenix must fall and rise again, with lightning tempest, and with rain. Seeker finds them, spirit binds them. Three are found, yet two remain." She nodded her head slowly to some inner rhythm. It appeared as if she was listening to something—or perhaps she was merely falling asleep. It didn't look as though she intended to speak again. Elissa was about to suggest to Maya that they leave when the old woman looked up and, in a clear, strong voice, spoke directly to Elissa. "*The birds will talk, and the earth will churn. The trees will walk, and the world will burn.* Mark my words! The End of the World is near. Go now! Find them! Om Chai has spoken."

Abruptly she rose and led the girls to the door. She made a sign of protection, twice, over the girls' heads and then pushed them into the street. Behind them the door clicked shut. Apparently the visit was over.

Elissa stood there for a moment, facing the narrow door. She had gotten no answers at all. If anything, she was left with more questions than she'd had when she'd arrived. Birds talking? Well, that was nothing new to her. It was hard to get them to stop. But trees walking, earth churning, the end of the world? It sounded more like a prophecy than an explanation. And what did the Phoenix myth have to do with anything? Not to mention that "Find them" was an odd piece of advice to give somebody who wasn't looking for anything. Elissa frowned so hard, her eyebrows hurt.

Maya did not seem at all perturbed. Her expression looked distinctly satisfied as she drew her veil across her face. Elissa thought she must have missed something important. She resolved to quiz Maya later, when they got back to her quarters and wouldn't be overheard. But in the meantime she wanted to make a detour.

"Maya," Elissa whispered. "I want you to take me somewhere on the way back. Is there time?"

Maya nodded.

"Take me to the stables."

Elissa couldn't see Maya's face, as it was completely covered by her veil. She didn't answer, in any case, but merely hurried along. Elissa was beginning to wonder if Maya had even heard her when she stopped before a high wooden archway. The unmistakable smell of horses told Elissa that she was in the right place.

"We can't spend too long here," cautioned Maya.

The stables were vast. The stalls seemed to extend endlessly before her. "How many horses does the Khan own?" asked Elissa incredulously.

"About four hundred. Whatever you want to do here, hurry," whispered Maya urgently. "I'll stay here. When it's time to go, I'll whistle."

Elissa hesitated. This was going to be an impossible search. Row after row of identical stalls stretched in front of her, defying her to find a single gray-nosed donkey. She'd have to do something drastic. Elissa drew in a breath—and brayed. Soon there was an answering *hee-haw*. Elissa smiled back at an astounded Maya as she trotted down the center aisle. "Farm trick. I'll be back in a moment," she called over her shoulder.

When she found Gertrude, sandwiched between a swaybacked packhorse and a lethargic mule, Elissa was so happy that she threw her arms around the donkey, nearly throttling her.

"Let go!" Gertrude grumbled, but she didn't look at all unhappy with the attention. She was still the same old Gertrude. "The food here is terrible," she said. "Way too dry. And they've housed me with the riffraff." But before Gertrude could gather up a full head of steam, Elissa interrupted her. She came straight to the point.

"I'm a woman!" she announced.

"Congratulations!" said Gertrude. "I thought you smelled different. How does it feel? You aren't with foal, are you?"

Elissa laughed. "No, Gertrude. Only the moon has touched me—nobody else. Besides, I'm just thirteen."

Elissa felt a hot, moist puff of air against her neck. She whirled around to find a pair of gorgeous, thickly lashed eyes staring into her own.

"Watch out, they spit," warned Gertrude.

"I never!" protested the camel. He gave Gertrude a hurt look and then gazed at her expectantly.

"Oh, all right," muttered Gertrude. "Elissa, Ralph. Ralph, Elissa."

Ralph inclined his head. The introduction was informal, but it seemed to suffice for him.

"I'm delighted to meet you," he said. "I've

heard so much about you from your charming companion."

Elissa couldn't suppress a giggle. *Gertrude? Charming?* she thought. Gertrude shifted from hoof to hoof, getting ready to either kick down the door or pee. She snorted expressively.

Elissa tried her best to look gracious.

"Gertrude has been a real addition to our group." Ralph batted his stunning eyelashes at Gertrude, who said nothing. "Well, I can see you two have a lot of catching up to do. Hope we meet again!" Then he ambled down the aisle, followed by a stablehand. Funny, Elissa hadn't noticed the stablehand before. He gave Ralph a push to get him going.

"Ralph can talk your ear off." Gertrude looked somewhat embarrassed.

Elissa cast a mischievous smile at Gertrude. "It looks like you have an admirer."

Gertrude humphed and hawed and clumped her hooves. "Camels!" she finally snorted.

Elissa heard a whistle. "I have to go, Gertrude dear. But I'll be back before you know it." She gave Gertrude another squeeze and kissed her soft gray nose.

Gertrude sniffed. "Bring me some real grass next time. These people know nothing about fresh greens." She looked at the hay in her stall with distaste. "This stuff is really stale." Then she shoved her nose against Elissa. "Missed you," she breathed. "Come back soon."

Elissa promised she would and ran down the aisle to where Maya was waiting impatiently. She turned around to wave at Gertrude as she ran. Gertrude snorted softly. It was a small, sad sound. As she passed Ralph's stall, the camel nodded politely. The stablehand who had shut the gate nodded as well. His hood was drawn down and his face bent low, though not quite low enough to hide the lightning flash of a smile.

"Let's *go,*" insisted Maya.

Elissa followed obediently, but something was bothering her. "Who is that man?" she asked.

"Just one of the stablehands," replied Maya distractedly. She had been thinking of how to keep her head attached to her shoulders. "He's new. What were you doing down there?"

Elissa didn't answer. Since last night she had been plagued by a haunting feeling of familiarity, like a half-remembered dream. It was as though she was seeing things she'd seen before, but couldn't recall where or when. That stablehand. Now, where had she seen *him*?

As the girls made their way back into the street, the stablehand's face broke into a broad, shark-toothed grin.

∽ 14 ∼

A Spy

The Khan found himself in a very fine mood that afternoon. His momentary discomfort at not receiving a sufficient number of pastries for lunch had been relieved by beating the cook, the servers, and a few guards, after which he had slept the deep, contented sleep of the justly vindicated.

The ancestors are on my side, he thought. *The side of Right.* The Khan needed very little proof of that. His superiority was obvious.

"I knew Kreel would prove useful," he said to himself as he picked up the white king. "Mate!" he exclaimed. It was so satisfying when he won. He clapped his hands together sharply, and when three blue-robed women appeared before him, he gave them his instructions.

"Bring her to me," he commanded.

The Khan rubbed his hands together with pleasure. *This time I am going to get it all—a new kingdom, a beautiful young bride, power, riches,* he thought. *The wonderful thing about possessions is that they have no limit. One can always get more.* The three women stood silently, waiting to be dismissed.

The Khan held up his hands to clap his dismissal; then a thought occurred to him.

"Bring the other one too, the little brown servant."

He clapped once and the women disappeared, their blue robes rustling like the sound of wind against sand.

The girls stole back to Elissa's quarters, pulling off their dusty outer robes as soon as they entered the room. Maya flung them into a corner.

"Made it!" Maya crowed in triumph. "And no one the wiser."

Elissa was desperate to get clean. Her robe had been stifling, and she felt sticky all over.

"Let's take a bath," she suggested.

Maya readily agreed. She would never turn down an opportunity to get into water. The two girls undressed hurriedly, dropping their garments onto the floor. When they got into the pool, Maya promptly disappeared.

"Maya? Where are you? Come up, Maya!" Elissa had never known anyone with the ability to stay underwater as long as Maya. The little girl's sleek head appeared at Elissa's elbow. She bobbed up and down. When Maya was in the water, she never stopped moving.

"Hold still, Maya! We need to talk." Elissa managed to grab a small foot as Maya swam by. "Listen." Her tone was serious. "What was Om Chai talking about?"

Maya squeezed her eyes shut, trying to organize her thoughts, which in Maya's case was not easy. Her mind, much like her body, never held still. "Om Chai can tell the past," Maya finally explained.

"Anybody can tell the past," said Elissa. "It's already happened."

"Not if they haven't been there to see it," countered Maya. "Om Chai sees everything. She is wise. So she doesn't always make a lot of sense to the rest of us."

Elissa had already had ample experience with

one wise woman who made no sense. Nana talked in riddles and rhymes, and told obscure tales—if she talked at all. And now here was another!

"What did she *mean*?" she cried. "Is the world going to end? Am I supposed to *do* something about that? What am I supposed to find?"

Maya's clear brown eyes looked deeply into Elissa's. "Sometimes it's better not to think too much." The girl looked suddenly older to Elissa, not like the child she was but like the woman she would become. "When the time comes, you will do whatever needs to be done," she said. "You will have no choice. Thinking about it won't make it any easier. Just float, Elissa. Everything will work out the way it's supposed to. It's in the hands of the goddess."

Elissa wished she shared Maya's conviction. "Let's get out. I can think better if you aren't splashing about." The two girls donned clean robes and entered Elissa's chamber.

They had visitors. Three blue-clad women stood in the center of the room. One of the women came forward and whispered into Maya's ear. She uttered only a word or two, but it was enough to make Maya's face grow pale.

"We have been summoned by the Khan." Maya's voice quavered. "We have to go."

"Can I change?" The robe Elissa was wearing was meant for sleeping. She would feel uncomfortable walking around in public without outer robes. Elissa cast a glance at the dusty robes Maya had flung into the corner.

One of the women made an abrupt gesture toward her, which clearly meant *right now*. Evidently the Khan did not like to be kept waiting.

As they walked down the hallway, Elissa whispered to Maya, "Why does he want to see *you*?"

Elissa was immediately sorry she had asked, for Maya's face had frozen in a mask of fear. "Don't worry," Elissa said. "I won't let him take you away." Maya looked somewhat reassured, but still she said nothing.

The Blue women led the girls into the Khan's audience hall.

The hall looked empty.

The two girls looked around themselves nervously. Maya turned to query the three women who had brought them, but they were gone. Elissa looked back over her shoulder at the double doors, expecting them to open.

"Welcome!" boomed a voice. The girls jumped. Apparently there was more than one entrance to the audience chamber.

The Khan stood before them, smiling, his enormous body swathed grotesquely in lengths of multicolored silk.

"You two have been out." He shook a finger at Maya. "Naughty, naughty." Maya trembled like a leaf.

The Khan never removed his eyes from Maya's ashen face and quivering body. "You know what happens to servants who disobey me," he said quietly, slowly drawing a finger across his throat.

Maya started to slump. The Khan watched her, smiling broadly. All at once his vision was blocked. Elissa had placed herself directly in front of Maya.

"Khan, it was my idea," said Elissa, her voice firm.

The Khan could not believe his ears. *"Idea?"* he said. "You don't have *ideas*. Only the Khan has *ideas.* Your only concern should be how to obey them. Your little adventures with this insubordinate slave are over. You are to be moved to the women's quarters—immediately."

Elissa felt Maya's twitch of alarm. She reached behind her to hold the girl's hand. It was ice-cold. "Maya will go with me," she said.

"No, she will not. She is a child. You must have a matron—suitable for a woman," he said in an insinuating tone.

Now it was Elissa's turn to feel alarmed. *How had he found out?*

"A little worm told me," said the Khan, reading Elissa's expression. "But enough chatter," he continued. "We will be married at sunset. You are of age."

Elissa's thoughts raced. *Who could have told him?* The only one who knew apart from Maya was Gertrude, and Gertrude couldn't tell anybody anything. Thinking about Gertrude jogged her memory. That stablehand . . . Kreel!

"At last I will possess Castlemar," the Khan gloated. He rubbed his damp palms together gleefully. "Nothing can stop me!"

"My father—" Elissa began.

"Is. Not. Here." The Khan was getting irritated. He was beginning to feel some doubts about this Elissa. Disobedient brides did not appeal to him. He clapped his hands twice. A set of burly guards entered the room. Three Blue women stood behind them.

"Take this one to the women's quarters," he said, gesturing toward Elissa. "Bring the other one to the executioner's block. And don't forget to serve refreshments."

The women seized Elissa, though not roughly. Maya wilted as soon as the guards touched her, and had to be half dragged from the room.

"I will see you tonight, my treasure," said the Khan. He left the room with a pleased expression on his face.

As she was led from the audience chamber, Elissa spotted a tiny movement in the balcony. It appeared they had a spy.

Elissa was deposited without a word in a small room on the other side of the palace. Apart from a narrow-slatted bench, the room was bare. She turned and tested the door. It was barred shut. She hadn't really expected the Blue women to leave it open, but it never hurt to check. Leading out of the room was a simple archway connecting to a larger room. She passed through it gingerly, not knowing whom to expect on the other side. To her relief, the room was unoccupied.

Her chambers had been nearly double the size of the room in which she currently found herself. But whereas her room had contained only a bed and chest, this one was filled with cots. They were crammed so tightly together, Elissa wondered how anybody got in or out of bed without disturbing the rest. She traversed the room to a second archway, only to find another room exactly like it on the other side. It seemed the Khan did not believe in pampering his women.

The thought of the Khan filled Elissa with disgust and anger. All at once her knees shook so badly, she sat down hard on one of the beds. How had she found the courage to stand up to that man? He was mad, that much was plain to see. Only a madman would think he could get away with stealing a princess. And now he had Maya! Elissa moaned out loud. She had to find a way out of here! She cast her eyes around the room, looking for irregularities in the tiling that might indicate a hidden door. Then she explored the floors for trapdoors, checking methodically under each one of the beds. The ceiling rose above her in a high dome, unbroken except for several small slits to let in light and air. Unfortunately, these were only a handbreadth wide. Apart from the entrance, there was no way out. She returned to the anteroom. The door was securely barred from the outside. Elissa tried to slide her little finger through the crack, but the opening was much too narrow. She needed some kind of tool to slip under the bar. Elissa turned her attention to the bench. The slats might be narrow enough. She tested each slat in turn, trying to find one that she could work loose.

She was almost finished prying up a slat when the door opened abruptly. Elissa sat down quickly, trying to hide her endeavor. One of the Khan's guards entered. Behind him stood three blue-robed women. Elissa had the feeling they were the same women who had accompanied the girls to the Khan's audience chamber. One of them was holding a black hooded robe in her hands. The guard indicated with a forefinger that Elissa should stand. Then he looked at the spot where she had been sitting and, grinning, pointed to the loose slat. For some reason the women seemed pleased. Their eyes crinkled as if they were smiling beneath their veils. The one with the robe nodded and stepped forward, holding the garment up by the shoulders. Apparently Elissa was supposed to put it on.

She slipped the robe over her head, wondering briefly if the Khan meant to marry her in servant's garb. Considering the size of his ego, she would have expected him to dress her in the most costly gown available. She pulled the hood over her head, planning furiously. She calculated that her opportunities to escape would be much greater once she had left the women's quarters. In the open she might be able to distract her guards and make a run for it. She figured that her chances of escape would increase if she could lull them into overconfidence, so Elissa stepped along meekly, keeping her head down, waiting for an opening. It seemed as though the women suspected her of planning something, for the three of them surrounded her so closely, she could feel their robes brushing against her. They passed by many doors and passageways, but none that Elissa recognized.

Elissa's heart sank. Her plan was flawed. Even if she could break free, she had no idea where she would run.

The passageway came to an end at a narrow wooden doorway. Judging from the smell wafting from the other side, they were at the stables. She looked at her captors in confusion. Getting married in servant's robes was one thing, but getting married in a stable was another. One of the women drew out an iron key and opened the door, which creaked loudly. The door was only wide enough for a single person. She invited Elissa to pass through, ahead of them.

Now was her chance! Elissa immediately bolted, only to run smack into a man who was waiting on the other side of the door. It was the burly guard who had carried Maya away. He grabbed Elissa by her arm as she tried to run past him. Elissa, in a burst of fury, fought him off, landing a solid kick on his shin that would have made Gertrude proud. As he released his grip in pain, she stomped on his instep for good measure and fled.

"Elissa! Wait!"

Elissa stopped dead in her tracks. The voice calling to her sounded like Maya's. She turned to face her captors, noting as she did so that none of them had given chase.

The guard she had kicked was rubbing his shin ruefully. Amazingly, the women were laughing. And even more to Elissa's surprise, they had dropped their veils. Their faces, as Elissa now saw, were strong and full-featured, and filled with pleasure. In front of them stood Maya, looking slightly shaken but otherwise completely unharmed. Elissa ran to her, hugging her tightly.

"Are you all right? How did you—? What— what happened?" she finally stammered.

"The guard brought me straight to the stables," said Maya. "The Blue People are going to get us out of here."

The guards and the three women nodded as Maya spoke. The guard Elissa had injured whispered something to the women, and they all smiled at Elissa. Elissa knew they were talking about her.

"They think you are brave," said Maya, "and clever. They like that."

Elissa didn't know if she should say "thank you" or "I'm sorry." But Maya continued talking, so she didn't have the chance to do either.

"They are going to hide us in their caravan. They're leaving tonight."

Elissa noted that the light was already beginning to wane. "Then we don't have much time."

"No, you don't," whispered a feathery voice. It was Om Chai! She was holding a bundle in her hands. Elissa noticed that Om Chai's robes were blue, like the desert people's.

"Not to forget," she said. She handed Elissa her traveling pack and the blue robe and long veil of the Blue People.

"More comfortable to travel in these than your night robe," she said, her eyes twinkling. So Om Chai knew she had been wearing her night robe in the audience chamber. Elissa remembered Kreel. He might be here, listening to every word!

"The spy, Kreel . . . you have to be careful. He's very clever," warned Elissa.

"Not to fear," said Om Chai calmly.

"But what about the Khan? Surely he will discover we are gone, and then—" Elissa shuddered

236

to think of what the Khan would do to her res-
cuers.

"Blue People will take you across the desert.
And Khan, he is . . . sleeping." Om Chai smiled
peacefully. Then her smile faded and her expression grew grim. "Days of Khan are few." From
the equally grim expressions on the Blue People's
faces, it did not sound as though Om Chai was
making a seer's prophecy this time, but rather de-
scribing an event that had already occurred.
"Now you must make ready to go."

"But how will we make it past the gates?"
asked Elissa. "Surely the gatekeeper will guess
who we are."

"Not to fear," the old woman repeated. "Gatekeeper is one of *us*."

As Elissa hurried into an empty stall to
change into the robes, she realized that the person in the women's balcony must have been Om
Chai. The ancient Tea Maker must have more
power than she thought. She wondered what else
Om Chai knew. She opened her pack. There was
a slightly wilted gardenia resting on top of her
belongings. Under it, her old skirt, cloak, and

blouses were neatly folded, and someone had even thought to replace her bootlace. She changed rapidly, shoving the black robe and night robe into the pack, but by the time she emerged from the stall, Om Chai had gone and a half dozen blue-clad desert folk had taken her place. She followed them down a side aisle to a courtyard where camels were being loaded up.

"We meet again!" Ralph bobbed his head happily. "These night voyages are so romantic, don't you agree? Especially with such charming companions." He swung his great neck around to gaze into Elissa's face.

"Don't you even *think* of spitting," grumbled a familiar voice.

"Gertrude! You're here!" Elissa was so happy, she spoke out loud, too loud.

"Well, of course I'm here. Do you think I'd let you leave without me?" Gertrude had been standing behind Ralph. She flicked her narrow tail stubbornly. "They'd better not try to make me carry anything. I'm not in the mood to walk around all night with a load on."

Ralph, ever the gentleman, ambled over to Elissa and knelt down for her to mount. She scrambled up to a thronelike seat. When Elissa was settled, Ralph turned to wink at her. "I *never* spit," he confided. "Not intentionally." He nodded his head amiably in Gertrude's direction. "Isn't she just marvelous? I love the way she just comes *out* with things! It's so refreshing."

In spite of Ralph's reassuring chatter, Elissa felt nervous. She glanced at Maya, who was perched atop another camel. Not until they were far, far away from here would she breathe easy.

The head man gave the signal to depart. The desert caravan proceeded majestically out of the main gate, into the red-stained desert. As the first star of the evening twinkled above them in the deep azure sky, Elissa made a wish.

❧ 15 ❧

Her Secret

After five days perched on top of Ralph, Elissa was beginning to wish she were anywhere else. Despite the fact that she was a man's height above the desert floor, she felt as though she were being dragged along it like a broom. Even under the cover of her long veil, her eyes were full of grit and her hair had turned to straw. Every swallow tasted of dust. Ralph, who was seemingly impervious to heat, grit, sand, and dust, politely checked on her welfare at every opportunity, which was to say every minute or so.

"Are you quite comfortable, my dear?" Ralph was nothing if not attentive. "Lovely morning, don't you think?"

Elissa nodded her head agreeably, even though the only thing worse than riding on top of Ralph would have been walking. But she didn't have the heart to chat, even though she knew nobody else could overhear her. Camel caravans, unlike horse and mule caravans with their companionable pairing, tended to straggle along single file, assuring them of complete privacy.

The caravan was following a southerly route. Elissa would not have thought it possible, but this low desert was even drier than the high desert she had crossed with her father to reach the Khan's Citadel. There was not a single shrub or tree as far as the eye could see. In fact, the more they proceeded south, the more spare the landscape became, until there wasn't any sign that the earth had ever sustained life on this hard, cracked surface. After they had traveled for seven days, the pebbly ground was replaced by sand dunes that Ralph patiently climbed and descended. It was like the sea she had heard about, with its endless waves billowing toward the flat horizon. And the sun overhead, always the sun. Even with travel restricted to early morning and late afternoon, it beat down on them like a fist. At last Elissa understood the reason for the voluminous clothing of the Blue People. In the low desert there was no mercy. Unprotected skin would crisp like one of Cook's fried cakes within an hour.

In spite of the heat and the huge emptiness of the desert, the caravaneers were in a fine mood, joking and calling to one another. The Blue People were on their way to the famed market of Alhamazar, to trade weapons and camels for cloth, spices, and copper pots. Alhamazar, the City of Spires, was located at the edge of the desert and served as the chief market for all the Southern Kingdoms. Consequently, it was a profitable destination—if dangerous. Wherever money changed hands, thieves and cutthroats abounded, a fact that disturbed the valiant Blue People not in the least.

Elissa and Maya would not be going to Alhamazar, however. Word had been sent ahead to Falk informing him of Elissa's escape. Tonight they would be transferred to a caravan heading east. Once they reached the desert's edge, a party of traders would be waiting to take Elissa and Maya to the western border of Castlemar. Frankly, Elissa was looking forward to the next leg of their journey. Though she would miss Ralph as a traveling companion, she would not miss the terrain.

As Elissa and Maya lay on their pallets that night, Elissa pondered her future. After she was reunited with her father, what then? Her escape had probably ruined his arrangements with the Khan. Would he be angry with her? Elissa wasn't sure that it mattered to her whether or not he was. Well, perhaps it mattered just a bit. He was still her father, no matter how little he cared for her. But because she was no longer useful to him, he would probably send her back to High Crossing. The prospect of going home produced mixed feelings in Elissa. The valley was familiar, and safe, but it was not a place where she could grow. Now that she was out in the world, she wasn't sure she ever wanted to go back. And what about Maya? She knew the girl should be returned to her people in the southern islands, but she would miss her terribly. Elissa fell into a fitful sleep. Toward morning she dreamt she was in Om Chai's smoky chamber. The old woman stood before her. She raised her palm, holding up her fingers. She touched each of them, wordlessly— as though counting. Then she bent three fingers down, touching the two remaining fingers. *Never fear*, she said. *The End of the World is near.* Elissa did not remember the dream when she awoke, but all day she was nagged by anxiety, as if she were late for something important.

Elissa and Maya bade farewell to the Blue People that morning. The eastbound caravan, a small group of horse traders who had been charged with the responsibility of taking Elissa and Maya to the desert's eastern boundary, had arrived the previous day. Ralph seemed heartbroken to be moving on without them.

"I shall miss you!" he cried. He bent down to say goodbye to Gertrude.

"Stop slobbering on me," she muttered.

"Gerty is not entirely comfortable expressing the softer sentiments," Ralph explained. "But I know that in her heart she cares."

"I'll get in touch next time I need a bath." She stomped off, flicking her narrow tail, grumbling in disgust. *"Gerty! Hmph."*

"She's even more beautiful when she's angry,"

murmured Ralph. Then he moved off to join the rest of the caravan.

After the Blue People had passed out of sight, Elissa felt her first small twinge of anxiety. The horse-trader caravan was not making any preparations to leave the oasis. Shouldn't they be loading up? From all appearances, it looked as though they had no plans to go anywhere. Some of the men were playing dice. Others were snoozing in the shade of the palms.

One member of the group, a man with a face like a hatchet, made even uglier by a jagged scar across one cheek, approached Maya and spoke briefly with her. These were not native desert folk but itinerant traders on their way up from Alhamazar, where they had exchanged horses for spices. Their manners were abrupt, so the leader did not chat long. Maya made her way back to Elissa. As with the Blue People, Maya acted as Elissa's translator. Elissa wondered briefly how Maya had accumulated so many languages. She didn't seem old enough to have had the time.

"The caravan leader says we are going to leave tomorrow," said Maya. Apparently Hatchet Face was the man in charge.

"Tomorrow? Why?" asked Elissa.

Maya shrugged. "He didn't say why—he just said we should go into our tent and wait."

Elissa wasn't sure what to do in these circumstances. She couldn't quite put her finger on it, but somehow the delay seemed suspicious. The leader would just as soon serve Elissa for dinner as talk to her, and his hard-eyed men did not invite conversation. The back of Elissa's neck prickled as she entered the tent. She was sure the hatchet-faced man was watching her.

At dusk Maya and Elissa ate dinner alone in their tent. They were more than happy to be left to themselves. The men were hardly fit company for two young girls. As the evening wore on, the band grew rowdy and argumentative. Elissa suspected that a bottle had been passed around—perhaps several. First the men hooted and howled with laughter, and then they yelled. Soon the yelling turned to scuffling. A couple of the men started shoving another against the back wall of the girls' tent, which bowed dangerously under the pressure.

"I don't like this," whispered Maya.

Elissa agreed. She was worried as well.

"Maybe we should bed down with Gertrude. They won't think of looking for us in the corral. And if they do, Gertrude's got a mean kick."

The girls gathered up their belongings and slipped out the tent flap. The horses were located on the other side of the oasis, but fortunately a grove of palms stood between their tent and the makeshift corral. If they hurried, they would not be seen.

Maya and Elissa scurried through the palm grove, keeping an eye out for watchmen. It seemed the corral guard was also drunk, for the gate had been left unattended. Elissa lifted the loop of rope from where it lay around the top of the gatepost and eased the gate open. Once inside, she breathed a sigh of relief. She felt safer among four-legged creatures. *At least animals know how to behave themselves!* she thought.

Gertrude was sleeping when they found her. Elissa and Maya laid out their blankets and stretched out beside her, glad for the peace and quiet.

Maya dropped off instantly, her head pillowed against Gertrude's side. Elissa, however, tossed about in her blanket. She didn't trust this lot. She reassured herself that tomorrow the caravan would be on its way, regardless of the bad behavior of the traders. However, in spite of all her efforts to remain confident, she could not relax. Her father must have gotten the message by now. If they were late, a search party would be sent. The thought comforted her. Elissa was just starting to fall asleep when she heard voices. She shook Maya awake.

"It's probably just the watchman," Maya mumbled sleepily.

"No, it's two people," insisted Elissa. "Something is happening. Come with me." Maya grumbled sleepily but complied. The girls crept close to where the voices originated.

Two men were standing by the gate. Elissa recognized one of them—the hatchet-faced leader who had spoken to Maya earlier. The man he was speaking with had his back to the girls. He was wearing a blue robe, and a long veil was draped around his neck. That struck Elissa as strange. She'd thought all the Blue People had departed that morning. Believing themselves to be alone, the two men didn't bother to lower their voices.

"What are they saying?" Elissa whispered.

"They're talking about us," Maya whispered back. "They've made some kind of deal."

"What deal?" Elissa was absolutely sure that whatever agreement the two men had reached, it wasn't going to be to their benefit. Also, there was something vaguely familiar about that Blue man. She wished he would turn so that she could get a good look at his face.

"Elissa, we've been sold as slaves!" Maya's voice shook. "The Blue man is paying for us right now!"

Elissa felt her heart sink into her boots. But in the next instant she remembered that the freedom-loving Blue People did not traffic in slaves. The Blue man was an impostor.

Elissa felt around until she found a small stone. Stealthily she heaved it into the palm grove behind them, where it made a small clattering noise. The Blue man turned, giving the girls a clear view of his face. It was Kreel! Somehow, Elissa was not surprised.

He must have hidden himself in the caravan, Elissa thought. He was right under our noses the whole time, where we would never have thought of looking. All he had to do was keep his face covered. She put her finger to her lips, signaling Maya to remain silent. Then, while the two men investigated the palm grove, the girls scuttled back to Gertrude. Elissa pulled at the sleeping beast's ears until she began to stir.

"We have to get out of here," whispered Elissa. "Now."

"Go away, Ralph. I'm trying to sleep," mumbled Gertrude. "You can tell me more dromedary jokes in the morning."

"Wake up, Gertrude! It's an emergency!" insisted Elissa.

Elissa poked Gertrude until the sleepy donkey cooperated, which was no small task. It took even more prodding to get Gertrude to tell her where the food supplies and saddlebags were kept. Then Elissa turned to Maya. The young girl was looking at her curiously.

"Maya, we have to get supplies together. If we leave now, we may be able to catch up to the Blue People. I'll get some food and water; you load up. Gertrude's trappings are over there." She pointed to a pile of saddles and bags by the fence.

Maya did as she was told, though her face still

wore a puzzled look. Elissa returned in short order, carrying several filled water bladders and two bags of dried dates and flat bread.

"These should see us through," she said. "Let's go."

The girls loaded up quickly and quietly. Guiding the sleepy Gertrude with their hands, they cautiously made their way to the gate. Nobody was in sight. Elissa opened the gate just wide enough to allow Gertrude to pass and signaled for Maya to follow. As the donkey picked her way delicately between the palms at the outer edge of the oasis, Elissa was trembling with fear, but she knew they had to move carefully. Kreel might be closer than they thought.

Silently they slipped from the haven of the oasis out into the open desert. However, Elissa's relief at escaping the encampment was short-lived. Behind them a shrill whinny pierced the night air.

"Alarum! Sound the trumpets!" cried the horse. "Alarum!"

Elissa was sure it was Kreel's horse—the coal-black gelding.

"Hurry!" she urged Gertrude.

"It's a good thing nobody understands him," remarked Gertrude. "It's that funny way he talks."

Elissa poked Gertrude in her side.

"Don't do that!" she said. "It's the middle of the night, and I'm not going to wreck my hooves in any high-speed races. I told you, nobody can understand a word he says. And besides, he bites. The other horses won't join in."

Elissa listened. It was true. Apart from a little snickering, the rest of the horses were quiet. Still, she was worried. While the desert would allow them to travel quickly, it would offer them no shelter or hiding place. What was more, she had no idea where they were going.

"I think we should head in that direction," offered Maya, pointing.

"How do you know that's the right way?" asked Elissa, peering into the darkness.

"It is," said Maya briefly. "I'm positive."

Elissa hesitated. They would die of thirst and exposure if they were so much as a degree off course.

The desert was completely silent, as though it

too were waiting. A brief burst of raucous, drunken shouting coming from the camp decided her.

"Let's go," said Elissa.

They headed off quickly in the direction that Maya had indicated. Elissa hoped that their absence would not be discovered for another few hours at least. With luck perhaps they could find another oasis, or an encampment of Blue People. She tried to reassure herself with all these thoughts as they trudged along.

The girls were both too exhausted to talk. Maya yawned and stumbled often.

"I need to sit down . . . for just a minute," mumbled Maya. "Just one minute." She began to slide down onto the dry sand.

"We have to keep going," urged Elissa. The encampment was out of sight, but there was no telling when the chase would begin. Poor Maya had slumped into a little pile, and her soft palace slippers, poking out from under her robe, were falling apart at the seams. Elissa grabbed Maya around the waist and hoisted her onto Gertrude's back. "And not a word out of you," she warned Gertrude.

Elissa walked beside Gertrude steadily, but as the long night wore on, she felt as though she were marching in place. The desert stretched out on all sides with not a landmark in sight. She walked with her head sunk to her chest, moving as mechanically as the gears of a clock. Every time she felt she could not take another step, she forced herself to remember Kreel's horrible gloating leer. Eventually she found herself sitting on the ground, Gertrude nuzzling concernedly at her neck. At that point she hauled the half-conscious Maya off Gertrude's back, and arranging the saddle blanket and bags, she made a bed for them.

Gertrude lay down beside them, her body forming a shield against the northern wind, which blew lightly but insistently against her flanks.

"Wake up." Gertrude was nosing Elissa, forcing her awake.

"I just fell asleep," she complained. Indeed, it seemed like only seconds had passed since she had closed her eyes. A few hours must have gone by, however, for it was light.

"Something's coming," said Gertrude.

Elissa leapt to her feet, looking for horsemen. But all she saw was desert and sky. On second thought, the sky looked odd. It was a peculiar mustard color. And it seemed lower than usual.

"Sandstorm," announced Maya. She was already up and loading their bags onto Gertrude. "We need to find shelter. Fast!"

Elissa cast her eyes over the empty landscape.

"Where?" There was nothing in her line of sight but sand and more sand.

"Just over that rise there is a small oasis," said Maya. She pointed to the south. "We need to keep the storm at our backs. If we hurry, we can make it before it catches up with us."

Elissa did not question her, though she did wonder how Maya could know where the next oasis was. But Elissa didn't have the time to think any more about it, for it was all she could do to keep up. Maya and Gertrude were traveling along at quite a clip. So was the storm. The wind was already picking up grains of sand and hurling them at her back, whipping her hair, and stinging her neck. She was glad they were not walking into the storm. Elissa wrapped her veil more tightly around her face and neck as she walked.

The girls kept up their pace, but the storm gathered strength behind them, forcing them to move faster.

"Hurry," pressed Maya. "It's catching up with us."

Elissa glanced behind them. The storm was advancing steadily. At this distance it looked like a huge churning wall that stretched up to the sky. When the wind hit, they would be flayed alive. Her breath rasped in her throat as she stumbled over the uneven terrain.

"We're almost there—keep going," urged Maya. Elissa could not see anything through her tearing eyes. Then she felt something catch the hem of her skirt. It was a fallen palm frond. Ahead she could just barely distinguish the outlines of trees.

"Help me gather up some fronds," shouted Maya. The two girls gathered up the long fallen fronds as quickly as they could. In the mounting wind they stacked and wove them between the slender, close-set palm trunks, forming a low wall.

"Get down!" Maya pushed Elissa to the ground behind the barrier and squeezed herself next to

Gertrude. Less than a minute later the storm hit. The two girls wrapped their arms around each other and pushed their heads down against Gertrude's side as the storm howled past them, throwing wave after wave of sand against the sheltering wall. They didn't speak; they couldn't. The steady barrage of sand and the howling of the wind kept them from uttering a word. They clung to each other as the wind threw the floor of the desert against their low wall, which tilted and sagged under the weight until Elissa thought they were going to be buried alive. Pressing their veils tightly against their faces, the girls crouched lower and lower until, abruptly, the wind died down. Then, covered in a blanket of sand, the girls slept in utter exhaustion.

When Elissa woke, the stars were out, shining tranquilly in the quiet night sky. Gazing upward, Elissa gasped. She had never seen so many stars. It seemed that the more she stared, the more she could see, until the black spaces between the stars seemed to disappear. Why, the sky was nothing but stars! Perhaps there was no sky at all. The little lights glowed and flickered like tiny flames.

Elissa began to feel unsettled. She sat up and

looked around her. Maya was curled up, fast asleep against a gently snoring Gertrude. Poor Maya—her feet were terribly swollen. It hurt Elissa just to look at them. Suddenly their situation struck her with the force of a blow. They were stuck in the middle of the desert with only enough food and water to last them a day—at most. A band of cutthroat slave traders was probably hot on their heels, and Maya couldn't walk anymore. She shook Maya awake.

"Do you know where we are?" Elissa asked. She tried to sound calm.

Maya looked up at the sky. "We are off course."

Elissa nodded. She'd already guessed. "We don't have enough water to make it," she said. She looked around the tiny oasis, searching for water, but all she saw was sand.

"This oasis is too small for a well," said Maya. "We'll have to head for the next oasis. It's about six hours' walk from here. South." She pointed.

Elissa was doubtful. "How can you tell? How do you know where the next oasis is?"

Maya thought. "I just know. I can smell it."

"You can *smell* an oasis?"

"I can smell water," said Maya simply. Then she began to arrange their packs.

Elissa stared at her. "When you said you sniffed out the Sacred Lake, I didn't think you meant with your *nose*! How can you do that?" she asked.

Maya looked straight into Elissa's eyes for a moment before she replied. "Well, I don't really do anything. It just comes naturally, like the way you talk to Gertrude," she said.

Elissa and Maya stood regarding one another. The moment had arrived—the one Nana had always warned her against. Elissa's secret was out. She had to confess that she hadn't been exactly careful about guarding it recently. What would happen if she broke her oath?

Looking down into Maya's open, trusting face, Elissa could not imagine there would be any harm in sharing her secret this one time. Maya would not condemn her, or fear her. She had a Gift of her own. They were a pair. For the first time in her life, Elissa felt she did not have to hide.

"Just don't tell anybody," she said. "It's a secret."

"Our secret," said Maya seriously.

Elissa smiled down at Maya. "I'm glad," she said. "Now I don't have to choose which one of my best friends to talk to. Well, are you willing to take a passenger, Gertrude?"

"As long as she doesn't kick me," said Gertrude.

Maya was waiting expectantly.

"Hop on," said Elissa. "Just don't kick."

"Is that what she said?" asked Maya.

"Yes, that's what she said."

Maya climbed up on Gertrude and patted her head. "Does she understand me too when I talk?"

"No," said Elissa. "But she knows you are kind."

Side by side they walked into the desert. The sky was starting to pale with the coming dawn. Elissa only hoped that Maya's ability to find water matched her own ability to converse with the beasts of the earth. Otherwise they would each carry their Gifts to the grave.

∞ 16 ∞

One Wish

"They've escaped again! It can't be!"

The traders looked on in amusement as the saw-toothed Blue man kicked furiously at the makeshift structure that had protected the two girls from the sandstorm.

Kreel howled and kicked for a few more moments. Then his beady eyes narrowed. He approached the hatchet-faced leader of the group.

"Give me back my money," he demanded. "I paid you for two slaves, and you have not delivered them to me."

The leader did not bother to reply. There was no need. His three silent companions had already spread out to form a semicircle around the impostor. Kreel quickly reassessed the situation. He smiled.

261

"Just joking," he said lightly. "How far is it to the next oasis?"

The leader did not return the smile or move his hard eyes from Kreel's face as he jerked his chin in the direction the girls had most likely taken.

"About two hours on horseback. Six on foot," he added. Then he signaled to the other three, and without another word they mounted their horses. As they left, they threw a bag of supplies and a water bladder at Kreel's feet. Tradition forbade leaving a man alone in the desert without a day's supply of food and water.

Kreel no longer cared about the loss of the money. It was not his anyway. He knew full well that the girls could not have gotten far. They were alone and on foot in a treacherous desert, and he had his horse. He pulled his hood over his head, smiling as he mounted his coal-black steed. Elissa would not escape him again.

The desert sun expanded until it filled the sky. And as it grew, the landscape around the girls seemed to shrink. In spite of the smoothness of the sand, the footing was uneven, slowing them down. Elissa had already fallen several times, and the gritty sand somehow always made its way into her boots no matter how tightly she laced them. Hours ago the girls had moistened their veils with a trickle of precious water and wrapped their faces and necks in the damp cloth in an effort to stay cool. Even this small respite was short-lived. Under the punishing heat of the sun, the moisture had instantly evaporated. At this point there was nothing left to moisten their clothing with—or to drink. They moved onward in a trance.

"How much farther?" Elissa panted.

Maya squinted at the horizon. "An hour," she whispered. "Not much more."

Maya had wilted over the course of the day. The relentless, scorching sun was sapping all the life out of her. She clung to Gertrude's back like an old rag doll. Gertrude didn't look much better. She walked slowly with her head drooping down. Elissa propelled herself forward on blistered feet, her eyes fixed on the ground before her. They stung with the salty sweat that poured down her forehead. Another hour seemed like forever.

Once again Elissa tripped and fell. This time she did not get up. It was so much easier just to lie there, as if she were floating. She dreamt she was in a stream with water swirling all around her; it was carrying her away to the sea. All she had to do was drift away.

"Is it ready to eat?" asked a voice.

"Almost," said another voice. "But don't dig in until it's tender. Last time you started when it was still moving, and the meat got tough."

"Well, it was *almost* dead."

"How many times do I have to tell you? *Almost* ruins the texture. If you want tender and juicy, you have to wait until it's *completely* dead."

Elissa opened one eye a crack. Vultures.

"I'm not dead yet," she muttered. "Be quiet." She willed the cool water to return.

"Lord love a corpse! It's talking!"

"She must be one of us, Vernon."

"Maybe she's Eugene's sister, the one who moved up north. You know the one I'm talking about. Mona."

"Mona? Is that you?"

Elissa opened both eyes. She was still in the desert. "I'm not Mona, I'm Elissa." Her lips cracked when she spoke.

The vultures squinted at her. "Do you know an Elissa, Edgar? I sure don't."

Elissa groaned. "Just do me a big favor. Go get help."

Elissa closed her eyes and tried to recapture the stream. She heard a snatch of conversation about Edgar's sister, who, it seemed, had married one of Eugene's cousins, Guy, who might have had a daughter named Elissa. Or was it Melissa? Then she drifted off into misty waterfalls and high pastures overlooking an emerald-green valley.

"Elissa, get up," said a little voice.

"I'm not Eugene's cousin's daughter," she mumbled. Her whole body felt stiff, and movement of any sort was impossible. She felt a tiny flutter next to her ear.

"Oh," whispered Elissa. The spirit was back. "Where have you been?"

"Get up." Then, miraculously, she felt something cool on her lips. Water! A single tiny drop.

She turned her head and saw that she had fallen within a few feet of a palm grove. Elissa rose on shaky legs and stumbled to the trees.

The sparse grove of palms stood dusty and tattered in the glaring sun. At its center lay a tiny puddle of muddy water. Maya lay on her stomach, looking at the mud. Gertrude lay beside her.

"I'm sorry," said Maya sadly. "There's nothing here."

"It's not your fault," whispered Elissa, crawling into the space between Maya and Gertrude. "You couldn't have known it had dried up."

"There isn't enough to drink, but we can dampen our veils." Maya weakly fingered the cloth around her neck.

Elissa hardly saw the point. She lay on her back between Maya and Gertrude and tried to think.

"Did you see two vultures?" asked Elissa.

"No," said Maya.

Hallucinations, thought Elissa. *Too bad.*

Maya was looking very weak. Another day on foot would surely be too much for her. And with no water and almost no food, the only way they'd get to the next oasis would be on wings.

"We just need to rest a little bit," Elissa said,

feigning a confidence she did not feel. "Gertrude can carry you."

Gertrude groaned.

A lead weight settled on Elissa's chest. She closed her eyes for a moment, fearing that they would give her thoughts away. She reached out to hold Maya's small hand in her own. The thin brown skin along the backs of Maya's fingers was cracked and abraded. She had so much to regret.

"Maya, if you could have one wish, what would it be?"

"I would like to return to the sea," said Maya simply.

Elissa gazed at her companion. *Poor little Maya,* she thought, *so far from her mother and her home. As am I.* She sighed. At least they weren't hiding from the truth anymore. They would share the inevitable together.

"And you?" asked Maya. "What would your wish be?"

Elissa thought briefly of the wish she had made only a short while ago under the desert sky. It was bad luck to tell a wish made upon a star, for then the wish would never come true. In this instance, however, she was going to die before her wish could be realized, so she might as well speak her heart.

"I wish my father loved me," she said softly.

Maya squeezed Elissa's hand weakly.

"He does," said Maya.

"No, he doesn't," whispered Elissa. "It's all politics with him. He doesn't really care about me at all."

Elissa tried to keep her voice neutral. She turned her head away from Maya to hide the pain. Even so, Maya heard the intense bitterness packed into Elissa's quiet statement.

"No, I *know* he loves you." Maya spoke as firmly as she could. If they were going to spend eternity together in this place, Elissa's spirit must not be angry.

"How?" Elissa turned to face Maya again.

"He said so," replied the young girl. "That day when I went to fetch him, I heard him talking. His uncle told him it would be hard to return if they lost the war."

" 'Uncle'? You mean Aldric?"

"Yes, Aldric. I thought he said 'uncle.' " Maya fell silent. She seemed to be drifting.

"Go on, Maya. What else did he say?" Elissa shook Maya's arm. "I have to know."

Maya drifted back to earth. "Aldric told your father . . . something else. Then your father said he regretted something. Then he said that he loved you."

"He said, 'I love Elissa'? Those exact words?" Elissa's voice quavered with intensity.

Maya nodded slowly. It was obvious that even the tiniest movement sapped her strength. "He said, 'I'll come back for her. She is my daughter and I love her.'"

Elissa took a deep breath, and the hard knot that had lain in her chest since the day Falk had told her his story dissolved. When Falk had come to her room, he had wanted to tell her something. He had wanted to say to her what he had told Aldric. She had suspected it, but she hadn't wanted to believe. If there had been any water left in her body, she would have cried.

"Oh, Maya," she whispered. "I have misjudged my father."

"Nobody has asked me yet what my wish would be," interrupted Gertrude. "I wish—"

"Gertrude, dear!" A familiar voice echoed through the trees.

"Ralph?" cried Elissa and Gertrude in unison.

The stately camel emerged between the palms. Gertrude rose to her feet braying, while Ralph slobbered all over her.

"Oh, my dear ladies, I have been so concerned for your collective welfare," cried the camel. "When I discovered you were in danger, I came as quickly as I could. I feared you had perished in that dreadful storm."

"How did you know we were in danger?" Elissa was dumbfounded.

"A pair of frightfully unattractive gentlemen conveyed your message in a very lengthy fashion," said Ralph. "But they meant well."

"I thought I was hallucinating," said Elissa.

"What is he saying?" asked Maya. "What were you hallucinating?"

" 'Two frightfully unattractive gentlemen,' " repeated Elissa. Maya tilted her head, uncomprehending.

Fortunately, Ralph had been loaded up for the journey to Alhamazar when the vultures told him of the girls' plight. Nobody noticed his absence in the chaotic bustle that always accompanies the departure of large caravans.

The girls drank the water gratefully and ate salted oranges and dates while Elissa told their story to Ralph.

"Ladies, I hate to insist upon haste in these circumstances, but we have very little time," Ralph said once they had gathered their strength. "The unattractive gentlemen informed me that another party was on its way to this oasis—your pursuers, perhaps."

Needing no further encouragement, the girls packed up immediately. The camel bent down. He wore an ample saddle on his back—and there was even a cloth for a canopy! The two girls clambered up, and for once Elissa was not sorry to be riding on his back.

"Gerty, darling, can you keep up?" murmured Ralph.

Gertrude was chewing on a date. She had revived considerably.

"For you, Ralphie, anything," she replied, batting her eyes.

Ralphie? Elissa laughed, or tried to. It came out as a wheeze.

"What are you laughing about?" asked Maya.

"I'll tell you later," panted Elissa. "I think Gertrude has gotten her wish."

Shortly before sunset, palms rose on the horizon. The Great Oasis, as Ralph informed them, was a central stopping point for all caravans heading south. Although the caravan the girls had left the Citadel with had moved on, another of the Blue tribes was now occupying it, which meant they would be treated hospitably. Ralph strolled casually into the grove, surprising a group of children who were playing at the desert's edge.

"Ladies," announced Ralph, "we have arrived."

Elissa had never been happier to arrive anywhere. A group of Blue People, all waving their hands excitedly, clustered around the camel in order to help the two girls dismount. They gestured and smiled, and with firm hands they steered them toward the main camp. Ralph and Gertrude were led away to the corral. Gertrude didn't twitch a hair at being separated from Elissa.

The girls were taken into a large tent, where a group of women went to work on them. They allowed themselves to be undressed and scrubbed with cloths that had been dipped in basins of rose-scented water. After their baths they were gently patted dry and wrapped in clean robes. A fragrant salve was spread over their blistered lips, cheeks, feet, and hands. Then they reclined on mounds of embroidered cushions while a small, curly-headed boy served bowls of spiced semolina and mint tea. Elissa believed she had never tasted anything as delicious as that simple meal. Afterward the girls stretched themselves out on soft rugs, too content to speak.

A sharp clap brought them upright. A man entered, accompanied by a dignified woman. She was wearing a plain white robe cut in the manner of desert women's garb, loose and wide-sleeved. Her veil was draped loosely over her head but not her face, and was held in place with an elaborate pin. When she straightened, she was nearly as tall as the man beside her. She regarded Elissa with unsmiling eyes under brows as sharp and straight as two arrows. There was something odd about her eyes. Unexpectedly, it was the woman who spoke first.

"Welcome to our home, honored guests," she

said. "I am Sohar. This is Jamil, the caravan leader. I hope you have been well attended."

Elissa was taken aback. The woman spoke perfect Common Tongue! "Yes, Mother, we have been very well attended," Elissa replied politely.

The woman smiled a little tightly at the title Elissa had given her. Then her face grew grave. She whispered a few words to the caravan leader, who stood silently at her side. He nodded.

"We would like to hear how you came to us," said Sohar.

Elissa told Sohar how the camel had rescued them at the oasis, in brief. She didn't give specifics about the vultures, though she did say that they had had unexpected help from some birds. Sohar nodded, looking not at all surprised.

"The djinns protected you in the desert," she said. "They look after . . . certain people." She fixed Elissa with her steady, direct gaze. Her eyes had a strange metallic gleam to them, as if they were covered with a thin layer of silver. They made Elissa shiver.

"But tell me," Sohar continued, "why were you at that oasis in the first place? None of the caravans have stopped there since it dried up. How did you become separated from your group?"

Elissa realized that she had left out the most important part of the story. Though Sohar's face remained calm, her lips tightened as Elissa described Kreel's deceit.

"It is a serious offense to impersonate a member of the Blue People, especially when dishonor is brought upon us," Sohar explained. "He will be dealt with. And as for the traders, they will no longer do business in this part of the world." Again she murmured a few words to the man at her side, and although her voice was low, there was no mistaking her tone.

Jamil unconsciously fingered the curved knife that glittered ominously at his belt. Watching the gesture, Elissa felt assured that Kreel would pose no further threat to them. Still, she wondered how she and Maya would arrive at their destination.

"Jamil's caravan is traveling to Alhamazar tomorrow. It will be safer and quicker for you to go by sea than to travel over land. So Jamil will arrange river passage from Alhamazar to Gravesport for you both. From Gravesport the barge captain will find a seagoing vessel to take you home. This time you will arrive safely. I will see to that," she promised.

Elissa knew that she could trust Sohar. It wasn't just the certainty in her voice, or the fact that Sohar was imposing. Sohar didn't look old, but there was an authority in her manner that suggested she was used to having people obey her. She was a woman who issued commands, not requests.

"Sleep," she said.

Sohar strode through the encampment, past the domed tents glowing orange with candlelight. She heard mothers murmuring to their children as they tucked them into bed for the night. A bat swooped down from a tree, ruffling her hair slightly.

When she came to the pale tent, she lifted the flap and entered. Glittering eyes fixed on her in the darkness.

"What news, Sohar?" whispered a voice.

"Two girls have arrived," said Sohar. "One with green eyes."

"Ahhh." The sound of sand blowing across the desert floor. "She has come."

"She is a *girl*." Sohar's voice was tight. "We need *men* to protect us. I have told her she will leave with Jamil tomorrow."

There was a rustling in the tent.

"She will not leave," said the voice. "She will stay until the battle is done."

❧ 17 ❧

The Ankaa

The next morning dawned clear and bright with promise. Elissa yawned and stretched luxuriously.

"Ooof," she said. She ached all over. If she hadn't known better, she'd have said she'd spent the night on a pile of rocks. She felt under her sleeping pad just to make sure. No rocks, just sand. Maya was still sleeping peacefully, her mouth slightly open. Then Elissa remembered.

"Wake up, sleepyhead!" She poked Maya with her toe. "Today's the day!" She gathered up her things hurriedly. "Wake up, Maya!"

Maya groaned and rolled over.

Elissa felt a pang of remorse. Maya still looked washed-out. And it wasn't like her to be so sluggish. Usually Maya was the one with boundless energy. Elissa knelt down at her side.

"I'll get you some food," she offered. "Wait here."

Elissa poked her head out of the tent door. It seemed everyone else was already up. Among the palms there were groups of women cooking around small fires, children playing at their feet. Elissa smiled. Children were the same everywhere, as were animals. She felt a slight tug at her skirt and looked into a pair of round, dark eyes framed by curls. It was the little boy who had served them last night.

"Mama says to fetch you for breakfast," he said. "I am the messenger." The little boy puffed up his chest slightly as he spoke. It was clear he was immensely proud of his tasks—fetching, serving. Elissa smiled.

He scampered off in the direction of the closest fire, Elissa following behind. It seemed that at least one family of desert people spoke Common Tongue. When she approached the women, they bowed their heads gracefully in a respectful salute and gently seated her upon soft cushions. Elissa was impressed by how clean and tidy everything was, even though they were cooking outdoors. It was as though they were inside their own kitchens, not right out in the open. Elissa looked up at the sky. *Maybe for them it is the same,* she thought.

The women served Elissa a bowl of sweet, milky gruel stewed with cinnamon and dates, accompanied, as always, by strong, hot mint tea. Just like the dinner the night before, it was delicious. When she said "Thank you" in genuine appreciation, they covered their mouths, shyly smiling behind their hands.

"Can I have a bowl for my companion?" Elissa addressed the one who appeared to be the boy's mother, hoping she would understand Common Tongue. To Elissa's relief, she did.

"Of course," she said, spooning out a generous portion into a bowl.

"Do you know what time the caravan is leaving?" Elissa asked as she took the bowl from the woman's hands. She noticed the backs of her hands were decorated with an elaborate design painted in red. Her fingers were long and delicate.

The woman's large dark eyes clouded. "No," she said. "Perhaps they will leave tomorrow."

Elissa's heart sank. "Oh, but Sohar said they were going to leave today for Alhamazar!"

A brief look of concern crossed the woman's face at the mention of Sohar. "Perhaps," she said. "Only Sohar knows." She turned back to her cooking with an air of finality.

Elissa walked slowly back to the tent, crestfallen. Why was it impossible for her to get anywhere? It seemed every step she took was a step backward. The little boy hopped at her heels playfully.

"What's your name?" Elissa asked.

"Muti," he said.

"That's a nice name," she said.

"It means 'obedient,'" he said. He smiled at her with a willing-to-do-anything sort of look.

"Would you like to do a task for me?" she asked.

Muti nodded and stood at attention. His dark, curly head barely reached her waist.

"Can you find Sohar? Tell her I would like to speak with her right away."

Muti trotted off while Elissa entered the tent with the bowl of food in her hand. She found Maya sitting up, looking groggy. Silently she handed her the bowl. While Maya ate, Elissa broke the news.

To her surprise, Maya seemed unperturbed. "We can't stay here forever," she said in a dull voice. "I'm sure they'll get around to leaving eventually."

"Eventually?" Elissa growled in her throat. This was not the response she was expecting. Where was the desire, the impatience, the outrage? "Don't you want to go home?"

Maya put the bowl down and slumped back into her blankets. Elissa immediately regretted her outburst.

"I'm sorry, Maya," she said. She patted her friend's head softly. "I'm just tired of the delays."

Maya smiled faintly up at her. "And I'm just plain tired," she said.

There was a little scuffing sound at the tent flap and a soft clap.

"Come in, Muti," called Elissa.

Little Muti scampered into the tent, quivering with excitement.

"The whole council wants to talk to you!" he said. "They want me to bring you right now!"

"Good!" Elissa's voice was emphatic. "Now we'll get some action! Are you coming, Maya?"

Maya groaned. "What for?"

"To help translate," said Elissa.

"You don't need me," said Maya. "Sohar speaks Common Tongue. And I'm tired."

Elissa frowned, worried. This wasn't like Maya.

"All right," said Elissa. "But try to eat some more of that while I'm gone." She pointed at Maya's bowl. It was still nearly full.

With Muti insistently tugging at her robe, Elissa left the tent. Except for a barking dog, the oasis was quiet.

"Warning!" said the dog. "Something is going to happen!"

That's good to know, thought Elissa. *But what?*

They crossed the oasis, skirting family tents and cooking fires. Women looked up as she passed but did not speak to her. It felt like the whole oasis was holding its breath. Muti trotted ahead of her, a man on a mission. But when they arrived at a large white tent, the little boy held back.

"I can't go in there," he said. "I'm not allowed. It's for Healers only."

"Healers?"

Muti held his palms up, as if to say, Who else?

Elissa didn't really want an explanation. Right now all she cared to know was when she was leaving.

She held out her hand and shook his small fist. With unexpected dignity, Muti bowed his head. Then he was gone. Elissa turned and entered the tent.

Inside, the tent was not as dim as her own goat-hide tent but softly lit from the sunlight filtering in through the loosely woven white cloth. A translucent white bowl had been placed in the center of the floor, around which a group of women sat. They held so still, they might have been made of stone. And like the tent cloth and the bowl, their desert robes were plain white. When she entered, the women stirred, although they did not rise.

"Welcome to the tent of Ankaa," said a woman with hair so white, it perfectly matched her robe. "Come sit with us." They shifted and made room for her. Elissa sat and wondered how to begin. She couldn't just blurt out "Why aren't you sending us home?" That would be very rude. But before she could say anything, all the women started to hum together—a single low note. She hadn't noticed anyone giving a signal.

"Let us become one," said the white-haired woman when the note died away. She had a very pleasant voice, deep and soothing.

The women in the circle reached around their necks, pulling up flasks that had been dangling under their robes on long strings. Elissa was reminded of the shard she carried around her neck and put her hand up to touch the little purse. It felt reassuringly warm. One by one, the women uncorked their flasks and poured the contents into the white bowl. They resumed their humming as they poured, and while each emptied her flask, the others sat so still, they seemed not to be breathing. But the hum seemed to grow louder, deeper, until all the flasks were empty. Then it abruptly stopped. The bowl was full, and now Elissa saw that the liquid was pink, glowing.

"Perhaps you are wondering why your journey

home has been delayed," said one of the women. Elissa looked up, relieved that someone else had brought up the subject. Sohar's odd silvery eyes looked across at her. It was she who had spoken. Elissa nodded.

"There has been a complication in our plans."

Elissa sensed that she meant something larger than sending a caravan to market, or sending her to Castlemar.

"We need you to stay a little while longer," she continued.

"How much longer?" asked Elissa.

The women looked at one another, not really conferring, just agreeing. Inwardly she groaned. Soon they were going to start speaking in riddles like Nana or Om Chai. They would say something like "until the desert churns," or "until trees walk," or "until birds talk."

"Until the birds speak," said one of the women.

"I knew it!" cried Elissa. "And the desert churns, and trees walk!"

To her surprise, all the women turned to face her, nodding and smiling. She realized with a small shock that every one of them had Sohar's silvery eyes. In the pale light of the tent they glowed like burnished steel.

"Then you will help us!" The white-haired woman spoke. In her voice there was a note of something darker than pleasure. Was it triumph?

"Help you do what?" Elissa's confusion was apparent. So was her reluctance. This was not the first time she had been informed of her obligation to do something she knew nothing about.

Sohar leaned forward ever so slightly. "She doesn't know," she said. She was addressing not Elissa but the white-haired woman. "Tell her, Tafat."

The white-haired woman, Tafat, nodded. So did all the others—in unison, as if they were all parts of the same creature.

"A long time ago," said Tafat, "the Citadel was ours."

"Your people built it?" asked Elissa.

"No, the Citadel is older than time," she said softly. "But we lived within its walls for centuries. We cared for it, tended its gardens, swept its streets, and honored the Sacred Lake. We followed the way of Ankaa."

"Ah," said Elissa. There was a thing or two she'd like to know about that Lake.

"Many came to us for our knowledge, and for the healing powers of the Lake, which we guarded wisely but not jealously, for no aid must be withheld from the infirm," said Tafat.

"So the Lake cures the ill?" Elissa thought Nana would like to know about this.

"The Lake strengthens the body, but it does not cure. Time cures. But we offered medicines, rest . . . peace." Tafat paused. "Hundreds came, perhaps thousands. And we served them all."

"You mean the Citadel was . . ."

"A sanitorium, yes, a place to heal. It was also a city—until the Old Khan arrived."

Elissa recalled Maya's tale. "You are the ones!" she said. "The Ankaa!"

"Some call us that," said Tafat, inclining her head slightly. "But we are only servants of Ankaa, the Divine Healer. We wait for her to come again."

Elissa frowned. "But that was a long time ago. Weren't you all killed?"

"Twenty thousand of us were," said Sohar. "It was sheer trickery. The Old Khan feigned illness.

But once he entered, he killed the Gatekeeper and opened our Citadel to his troops. Only nine of us escaped the massacre. We were traveling to bring the healing waters to the ill. If we had been in the city that night, we would have been killed as well."

Elissa looked around. There were only eight women in the tent. She remembered where she had seen their simple white robes before.

"The Khan's mother," she murmured. Sohar nodded.

"And Om Chai?" asked Elissa. Surely Om Chai must be a Healer.

Sohar smiled slightly. "Om Chai is Om Chai," she said, which told Elissa exactly nothing.

Something was bothering Elissa about Sohar's story. She counted in her head. "I thought it was the Khan's great-grandfather who invaded the Citadel. You must not have been born yet."

"We were much as you see us now," said Sohar.

Elissa looked at the bowl of shining pink water. "The Lake! It made you immortal." She was mortified. She had not only drunk that water, she had swum in it!

But Sohar was shaking her head. "No, the Lake does not grant immortality. Not even in the quantity you managed to swallow." She raised her eyebrows knowingly. Elissa had the feeling that as far as the Lake was concerned, she had no secrets. Or perhaps she had no secrets as far as Sohar was concerned. "But it does slow the pace of aging if you take the waters on a regular basis. Say, every day for a hundred years or so."

"You're one hundred?" Elissa squinted at the Healers, the ones who remained silent. Most of them gazed back at her with eyes nested in wrinkles. If Sohar was a hundred years old . . .

"One hundred twenty-eight," said Sohar.

Elissa gasped. *Then how old were the rest of them?*

Tafat cleared her throat. She waved a finger at Sohar. "Enough," she said.

"We have been planning for four generations to take back what is ours," continued Sohar, getting back to business. "The first Khan captured a Blue woman and forced her into marriage, thereby securing the loyalty of the tribes. But all loyalties become strained over time, especially those that are one-sided. Finally one of us made the sacrifice of marrying the current Khan's father." She pressed her lips together in a delicate gesture of distaste. "Afterward it was fairly easy to replace the Gatekeeper and certain key palace staff with those who were loyal."

"Blue People?" Elissa was beginning to understand.

"Yes," said Sohar, nodding. "We have served the Blue tribes for centuries, far better than the Khans. And they, in turn, protect us. It was Om Chai who helped us locate you, of course."

"Me?" asked Elissa, startled.

Now Tafat spoke. "I saw you in the waters," she said. "Many years ago. A young woman with eyes like new leaves would enlist the aid of the Earth, and her humble creatures, to help us."

"But how can I help you?" protested Elissa. "The Citadel is days away. Surely you don't mean for me to return there?"

The women's laughter rustled through the room like dry leaves rattling in the trees in autumn.

"No," said Tafat. "That won't be necessary.

The Khan has been expelled. The Blue People evicted him the night you left."

"You see," explained Sohar, "the Khan lent your father his crack troops—his palace assassins. Once they were gone . . ." She spread her hands and there was more laughter.

"Foolish Khan. Arrogant Khan." The Healers put their heads together, their dry voices crackling with delight.

Elissa fidgeted impatiently. "But why do you need me? It seems like you've handled the situation just fine by yourselves. You've got your Citadel back, and you'll never see the Khan again."

The laughter ceased abruptly.

"I am afraid we shall be seeing him very shortly," said Sohar. "The Khan is coming here—with an army from the Steppes. He will seek vengeance against us for daring to defy him, just as his great-grandfather did."

The Healers watched Tafat expectantly. The old woman took the bowl in her hands and, holding it in her lap, gazed raptly into the pink waters. Elissa saw the reflection of the waters swirl across her face, illuminating her wrinkled cheeks and chin. When Tafat lifted her eyes, they were blazing red. In her eyes Elissa saw the flames, the oasis burning, the downward-arcing swing of the sword. Then eight pairs of eyes turned to Elissa, gazing at her intently. All her life Elissa had guarded herself, and her secret. She had wrapped herself in a cocoon of invisibility. But now she was being asked to emerge, not for her own sake but for others. It was time to share her Gift. Elissa straightened her shoulders.

"Just tell me what to do."

⇜ 18 ⇝

The Prophecy

At Elissa's insistence Sohar accompanied her back to the tent once the meeting was finished and the healing waters redistributed.

"She's quite sick," explained Elissa. "She can hardly move."

The tent flap was down, an indication that Maya had not gotten up yet. Elissa glanced at the sun. She'd been in the Healers' tent for at least two hours. There wasn't a sound from within. Elissa lifted the flap, now very worried.

Sohar hurried over to the huddled shape on the floor. She turned Maya carefully onto her back, feeling the skin on her neck and hands. Maya moaned softly when Sohar gently pulled down her eyelids.

"Why didn't you tell me?" Sohar's voice was sharp. "This child is nearly passed."

Elissa's blood froze. "What do you mean?"

"Raise her head." Elissa squatted beside Maya's pallet and lifted her head. Maya did not respond at all.

Sohar slipped the flask from around her neck and held it to Maya's lips. "Tip her head back." She poured the tiniest amount of liquid from the flask, just enough to wet Maya's lips. Maya made no effort to lick them.

"A little more," said Sohar.

Elissa dropped her hand a little. Maya's head rolled slightly, loose on her neck. Her eyes were completely sunken into her wan face.

"Oh, Maya," she whispered. "Please don't go."

Sohar parted Maya's lips with her finger and poured a thimbleful of liquid into the corner of her mouth. She turned Maya's head to the side.

"Now put her head down," said Sohar.

Elissa lowered Maya's head gently to the pallet.

"Will she be all right?" asked Elissa. Her chest was so tight, she could hardly speak.

"Perhaps," said Sohar. "We'll wait a few minutes and then try again. Her name is Maya?"

"Yes," whispered Elissa.

"The desert is very hard on water children."

"How do you know she is a water child?"

"Her name means 'water,'" said Sohar, as if no further explanation were needed.

Sohar fell silent, focusing all her attention on Maya. Elissa peered down into Maya's face. It still looked ghastly.

Sohar gestured to Elissa, and they repeated the procedure. Maya choked and gasped.

"Ah!" said Sohar. "Progress!" She poured a few more drops into Maya's mouth. This time Maya opened her eyes.

"Where am I going?" Her voice was very faint.

A sob of pure relief escaped from Elissa's lips. "Nowhere," she whispered. "Nowhere at all."

"Now she can drink some water," said Sohar, sitting back. "Lots and lots of water—with this much sugar in each cup." She held her palm out, making a small depression in the center. "Feed her a little bit at a time until she can sit up and drink on her own. Then she can have weak tea and later some broth."

Elissa nodded.

"When she can sit up, come see me." Sohar stood up rather abruptly. Her body was taut with anxiety.

"I will," promised Elissa. She was worried too, for once the Khan arrived with his forces, it wouldn't matter that Maya was cured. They would all be burnt to ashes. And as if that weren't gruesome enough, her next thought was even more troubling.

Those who survive will wish they hadn't.

To Elissa's immense relief, Maya recovered quickly. After a day she was sitting up and drinking tea. She was even playing a little with Muti, who was stretched out beside her on his stomach.

"I have to go meet with the council," said Elissa.

Maya raised herself up as if she intended to follow.

"No," said Elissa, pushing her back gently. "You stay here with Muti. He'll fetch what you need." Muti nodded his head vigorously. "This is something I have to do alone."

Elissa made her way through the camp,

wondering what would be expected of her once she arrived at the white tent. She found Sohar waiting for her by the tent flap, alone.

"The others are reading the waters again," she said tersely. "How is the little girl?"

"Much better," said Elissa, beaming. "She's eating a bit."

Sohar's austere features softened into a smile. "Good," she said. To Elissa's surprise, she held back the flap so they could enter together.

The Healers were gathered around the bowl. They leaned back when Sohar and Elissa entered.

"He's on his way," said Tafat. She looked pointedly at Elissa.

"We'll need to find out where he is and how many soldiers are with him," said Sohar.

"Don't the waters tell you that?" asked Elissa. *What good is seeing the future if all you get is what you already know?* she thought.

Sohar smiled wryly. "The devil is in the details," she said. "Perhaps you can help us with those."

Elissa nodded her head. "I think I can," she said, rising to her feet.

Sohar accompanied Elissa out of the tent. The prophecy about the talking birds had given Elissa an idea. She looked up at the sky. Following her lead, Sohar looked up as well. The sky was perfectly clear. Looking down again, Elissa spied a small movement from the corner of her eye.

"Muti!" she called. True to her hunch, Muti popped out from behind a bush. "You followed me! Aren't you supposed to be attending to Maya?"

Muti grimaced. "My mother is feeding her," he said. It was clear from his expression that he did not consider hand-feeding to be an important job. "This is more fun."

"Ah," said Elissa. "Then can you fetch me a heavy cloth?"

Muti bounced off, happily humming to himself.

"How do you get more water from the Sacred Lake?" asked Elissa, shading her eyes against the sun. "I mean, it's been a hundred years since you left. Didn't you run out?"

"The Blue People bring it to us," said Sohar. "In their caravans."

"Oh." It was obvious, really. But someone had to go down to the Lake, risking death to get it.

"Om Chai arranges it," said Sohar, again reading her mind.

The mysterious Om Chai.

"What are you looking for?" asked Sohar. She peered upward, trying to see something other than sky.

Elissa didn't answer, for just then Muti ran up, breathless. He was grasping a thick piece of cloth in his little hands. When he reached Elissa, he held it before him like an offering.

Elissa glanced down just long enough to take the cloth from him. "This will do," she said, draping it over her arm. She wrapped it twice. "Thank you, Muti."

"What are you looking for?" repeated Sohar. At this point all three of them were looking up.

Elissa screamed.

It was not a human scream. Muti covered his ears. Within seconds a dark shape plummeted out of the sky. Muti ran for cover. Even the fearless Sohar stepped back. A few feet above Elissa's arm the young eagle brought himself up short.

For a moment or two he blotted out the sun. Then, with a whoosh of huge wings, he settled. Elissa stumbled under his weight.

"Hello," said Elissa.

"I was hunting," said the eagle, a little irritably. He cocked a speculative eye at Muti. "Got any food?"

"I am sure something can be arranged," said Elissa. She'd make sure Muti wasn't around for lunch. "Can you do me a favor?"

"Will it take long?" asked the bird.

"There is a large group of people coming from the north," she said. "I need to know how many, and where they are."

"Numbers," said the eagle, "are for humans."

"Don't worry," said Elissa. "I'll help."

"Food?" asked the eagle, fixing his yellow eye on her.

"Afterward," said Elissa.

"All right then." The eagle dipped his head.

Elissa lifted her arm high, and with a leap that nearly knocked her over, the eagle took off. His wing tips brushed the ground lightly, leaving scuff marks in the sand.

"Aaaii!" cried Muti.

Elissa reached down to comfort him.

"That was the *most best* thing I ever saw!" Muti jumped up and down in excitement. Then he careened off to tell his friends, holding his arms out from his sides like a bird, screeching.

Sohar had lost her composure when the eagle had landed, and her face had yet to regain its customary severe lines. Under the softening effect of awe, she looked almost beautiful. Elissa smiled to herself.

"We'll have our answers within the hour," said Elissa, dead sure. "I promised our scout we'd have some food ready." She wanted to make certain the eagle did not choose his own meal.

Sohar glanced up at the sky. "I will arrange something," she said. "Is there anything else you need?"

"I forgot to tell Muti to bring a sack of beans," said Elissa.

Sohar nodded her head and walked away.

Elissa did not move from her spot. She had never called an eagle down before. Frankly, it made her a little uncomfortable. She was not in the habit of using animals for her own purposes.

Mostly she just appreciated their company. At this moment she wasn't sure she enjoyed involving them in human concerns. But she comforted herself with the thought that as long as the creatures weren't hurt, it should be all right. Besides, the eagle was getting a free meal. Elissa felt a pang of regret. She knew what eagles ate.

Sohar returned. "We shall offer him an old goat," she said. "It's at the edge of the oasis." She placed the sack of beans at Elissa's feet.

Elissa nodded her head. The facts of life could not be escaped. There was sickness, and there was death. Once again she turned her eyes to the sky. Within a few moments a dark spot appeared, so high it looked like a speck of sand thrown against the sun. Elissa tightened the cloth around her arm.

This time there was no scream. The whoosh of powerful wings caused Sohar to lean back, but she held her ground admirably.

Elissa braced. The eagle landed gently.

"Better this time?" asked the bird.

"Much," said Elissa.

"Don't get used to it," said the eagle.

"Did you see them?" asked Elissa. "Where are they?"

The eagle cocked his head and described a ravine flanked by scrubby trees. "It's a good place to hunt rabbits," he said.

Elissa relayed this information to Sohar.

Sohar looked dismayed. "That's very close," she said. "Less than six hours. How many?"

"Throw some beans on the ground," said Elissa. Sohar cast her a puzzled glance but obliged.

"How many of them?" asked Elissa, scuffing her feet beside the beans.

Again, the eagle cocked his head this way and that. "More," he said.

"More beans," said Elissa. Sohar threw out another handful.

"More," said the eagle.

Elissa nodded, and Sohar threw out another and yet another. Then two more.

"That's about right," said the eagle.

"Now count the beans," said Elissa. Her arm was getting tired.

Very quickly, in groups of ten, Sohar added up the beans. "Seven hundred." She blew a puff of air from between pursed lips.

"Seven hundred men?" asked Elissa.

"If you say so," said the eagle. "But they looked like horses to me."

"On horseback," said Elissa.

Sohar groaned. "Cavalry," she said. She sank her head in her hands.

"Where's my food?" asked the eagle.

"On the other side of the oasis," said Elissa. "And thank you."

With that, he rose majestically from her arm.

Elissa let her arm drop in relief.

Sohar's eyes were fixed on the beans. "We have eighty-five people at the oasis," she said. "Eighteen men. Twenty-two women. Forty-five children." She turned desperate eyes to Elissa. "And they're so close! There is no way the other Blue tribes can get the word in time."

"Where are the others?" said Elissa.

"It would take a day for them to reach us," said Sohar. "Six hours there and six back, on horseback. By then it will be over." She pressed her fists tightly against her stomach, as if in pain. "Why didn't they *listen* to me?" she groaned. "I *told* them not to wait! I told them to send the message two days ago. But they are too fixed in

305

their ways. They relied on *you*." Sohar fixed her hard gaze on Elissa. "And now it's too late."

"Don't be so sure," said Elissa. She was looking up at the sky again. "If you can get the message, I'll get the messengers." Sohar looked up then and saw what Elissa saw. Without a word she gathered up her skirts and strode swiftly back in the direction of the white tent.

Elissa made her way to the far end of the oasis. Women stopped stirring their pots, children paused in their play. She wondered where the men were. Probably sharpening their knives. As she passed, each and every one of them lowered his or her eyes in respect. News travels fast.

Elissa walked through scented groves of almond and pistachio. She didn't hurry. The last thing she wanted to see was the final moments of that poor goat. If she walked slowly, then by the time she arrived, the eagle would be done. And the messengers would be arriving.

She passed beyond the welcome shade of the trees and faced the open desert once again. There was a stake and an empty tether a few yards from the perimeter of the oasis. Beside it lay the bloody remains of the goat. The eagle was gone.

A few vultures landed even as she watched. They hopped to earth in their awkward, lurching dance, close enough to the corpse to smell it but far enough away to take flight in case some other predator was lurking near.

"Edgar," she called. "Are you out there?"

The birds stopped hopping for a moment. The truth was, she couldn't tell one vulture from another.

"Look, Edgar!" cried one of the birds. "It's Eugene's sister, Mona."

"No, you half-blind bag of feathers, remember? Mona's up north. That's Guy's daughter . . . I forget her name."

"Elissa," said Elissa.

"Yeah, that's right, Elissa. So how's Guy doing?"

Elissa decided it wasn't worth the effort. "He's fine," she said. "Could you do me a favor?" she asked.

"Didn't we do a favor for you before?" asked the vulture who might be Edgar. He hopped closer, suspicious.

"Yes," said Elissa cautiously.

"Oh, good," said the vulture. "That was fun. Remember, Vernon? We met that nice camel."

Sohar arrived short of breath, Muti following close behind. Elissa didn't see anything that looked like a letter.

"Are these the messengers?" Sohar asked, incredulous.

"Yes," said Elissa. "Do you have the message?"

Sohar rolled up her sleeve. Arranged on her arm were eight silver bracelets. They glittered in the sunlight.

"Ooooh," said the vultures.

Sohar began to slip the bracelets off. She held one up to Elissa.

"This is our pattern," she said, running her finger over an interweaving design along the edge. "Only the Healers wear these bracelets. When the tribesmen see these, they will come immediately."

"How many Blue tribes are there?" asked Elissa.

"Nine in all," said Sohar. "But one tribe is in the Citadel and one is here."

"Seven, then," confirmed Elissa.

Sohar nodded. She dangled seven bracelets from her hand. The eighth remained on her wrist. Elissa looked over the vultures, counting heads. There were more than enough for the job.

"Are there seven of you who would like to make some deliveries?" She held up the bracelets and jangled them.

"Pretty," said the vultures, hopping closer.

"I only need seven," said Elissa.

The birds quit hopping. They eyed one another.

"How about it? Edgar, Vernon?"

"Yeah, but if we go, the others will get everything."

Still holding the bracelets in the sunlight, Elissa turned her head. "Muti, how would you like to guard a carcass?" Muti nodded his head. He ran to fetch a stick.

"That boy there will protect the . . . food until you've all come back," said Elissa, pointing to Muti's retreating back.

Elissa handed out seven bracelets. "Do you know where the people have their camps?"

The vultures cackled.

"I suppose you do," said Elissa. Vultures always

kept a close watch on herders. "Each of you go to a different camp. Take a bracelet and drop it on the first person you see there."

The birds flew off, bracelets dangling from their beaks.

"They won't be long, will they?" asked Sohar anxiously.

"No," said Elissa. "They want to eat." She looked at the goat carcass. Muti was standing over it with a large, well-worn stick. It was a law of Nature. There were those who ate and those who were eaten. There was no point mourning it; the laws of Nature were unalterable. But the laws of Man—those that governed war, conquest, and subjugation—were not.

"Let's go back," said Sohar. "The others are waiting."

The two of them walked back through the oasis silently, although Elissa thought she detected a change in Sohar's attitude. She frequently looked back to see if Elissa followed, and there was a softness in her glance. When they came to the white tent, she waited, holding the tent flap aside.

"You first," she said.

Elissa entered. Fourteen glittering, metallic eyes met hers.

"Your message has been sent," she said.

"Ahhh." They all breathed out at once. "Come, come."

This time they did not make room for her. Sohar nudged Elissa forward until she was in the center of the circle.

Not knowing what else to do, she sat.

"It is time to finish," said Tafat. She held the white bowl before her in both hands. It was still glowing pink. "The prophecy will soon be fulfilled," she said quietly. "And our waiting will be over. Once again the Citadel will be ours." The women began to hum.

Tafat took a sip from the bowl and passed it to the next woman, who also took a tiny sip. The bowl made its way around the circle, each woman taking a small sip. When it returned to Tafat, she lifted it up, touched the bowl to her forehead, and passed it to Elissa.

"Drink."

Elissa took a small sip.

"More."

Elissa took another sip.

The women hummed.

"More."

Elissa looked at Tafat. She wasn't sure she wanted to live *that* long.

"You will need all your strength," said Tafat. "Finish it."

Elissa looked into the bowl resting between her hands. The water swirled, staining the rim pink. She raised it to her lips. She didn't know how much strength she had, but she knew that defeating the Khan would take all of it. She drank long and deep. She tipped back the bowl until there was not a single drop left, swallowing the waters of the Lake to the drone of a thousand bees.

∞ 19 ∞

Her Siren Call

It was late afternoon, that time of day when the sun pours its honey over the earth in long, sweet strands. Maya was looking much better, although she was still weak.

"You don't have to do this," she said.

Elissa turned to face her. She'd been admiring the sunlight, the way it streamed through the trees and made the dust on the horizon turn red.

"Yes, I do," she said. Elissa had taken off her desert robes and donned the clothes she had been wearing when she'd left High Crossing. Her drab homespun skirt and linen blouse looked as out of place here as desert robes would have looked in the far north.

"You can wait for the tribesmen to come, can't you?" asked Maya. Her eyes stared up from the pallet, little pools of darkness. "They will be here soon."

"Of course they will," said Elissa. She was waiting for Sohar to come. The other Healers would already be there, standing in a line at the edge of the oasis, watching the dust on the horizon draw close.

Elissa crouched down beside Maya. She put her hand on Maya's forehead. It was cool.

"Everything is going to be all right," she said.

Sohar's sure step roused her from her thoughts. Elissa kissed Maya on the forehead and rose to leave. She smoothed her skirt and straightened her blouse. Then, before she passed through the tent flap, she leaned over and, in a swift movement, pulled off her boots. She wriggled her toes on the rug.

I have good feet, she thought. *Good, strong peasant feet.* Then she stepped through the flap.

As soon as her feet touched the ground, she felt it. A deep subterranean vibration. It flowed up from the earth into her body.

All my strength, she marveled. *It was here all along.*

The air that hung over the oasis was slightly

hazy; motes of dust twinkled in the slanting sunlight. The cooking fires had been left unattended, and thin wisps of smoke curled lazily from under abandoned pots. There wasn't a soul in sight. Elissa and Sohar walked through a stand of orange trees to an ancient olive grove, the scarred trunks rising above masses of gnarled roots. Elissa briefly touched the bark of the nearest tree as they passed. High in the branches, the silvery leaves quivered slightly.

The entire population of the Great Oasis had gathered beside the olive grove in ranks. Closest to them were the women and children. Before the women stood the men, and before them, in a semicircle, stood the Healers. The men gripped curved knives in their hands, the women frying pans. The children clutched rocks. Judging from the determined expressions on their faces, they all intended to use their weapons. Only the Healers stood empty-handed. When they saw Elissa, they turned to her as a body. Sohar walked with Elissa to the front of the line. Tafat turned to her.

"Well, Daughter," she said.

"Well, Mother," Sohar replied. Sohar reached out and touched the old woman's hand. Her fingers were trembling. There was something wistful in the old woman's expression, tenderness mixed with the defiant courage of a sparrow defending her nest against a plundering crow. Elissa recognized it as love.

They stood, waiting, saying nothing to one another. Elissa knew that they were waiting not just for the ranks of soldiers to descend on them, but for her. She felt the ground tremble slightly beneath her feet and turned away from the women, who had already given over a lifetime to waiting and many lifetimes to serving.

The dust the army had raised seemed to thicken on the near horizon, which, in the late-afternoon sun, wavered with the illusion of water. Elissa squinted, straining to make out shapes. Then the horsemen appeared, galloping at full tilt over the small rocky rise that separated the oasis from the broader expanse of desert beyond. File after file of horses, their hooves pounding the desert sand to fine dust, came charging over the hill. Elissa felt the Blue People shift behind her. The Healers did not move a muscle.

When the cavalry reached the base of the hill, they came to a full halt. The hard-faced riders sat quietly on restive horses, holding their glittering swords at the ready. As far as the eye could see, there was nothing but war machine.

It's a beast, thought Elissa. *And the swords are its fur.*

"Why don't they attack?" she asked.

"The soldiers won't attack until they receive the order," said Sohar. "The Khan has not yet arrived." Sure enough, through the miles of kicked-up dust, Elissa made out a wagon struggling up a distant incline. "We must wait."

Elissa looked back over her shoulder. She spotted a woman clutching a baby. The woman gave her a tiny, nearly imperceptible nod, her eyes gleaming with desperation and strength. It was Muti's mother. She would die defending her children. And the men would die defending their women. And the Healers, in the front line, would die defending them all. And the children would simply die.

"I'm not waiting," said Elissa.

She had taken the first step before she realized what she was doing. In a sort of trance she moved forward. The desert floor was rough and hot against her bare feet. It was like being licked by a cat. Under the dry surface she felt something quivering, alive. As she approached the line, her heart began to beat wildly against her ribs, like a bird struggling to free itself from a cage.

The soldiers watched impassively as a slender girl with a full skirt and white blouse advanced toward them. The horses, dressed for war and shielded with blinders, shied nervously as she approached. Elissa stopped before a soldier. With his sword, mustache, and hard eyes, he looked like all the others.

"Go away, little girl," he said. He didn't look at her.

"I wish to speak with the Khan." It was hard to get the words out. Her mouth was a desert all its own.

The soldier looked down. "You will die soon," he said. "Go back."

Elissa's heart knocked. "Don't you have a mother?" she asked.

The soldier's eyes were cold as ice. Perhaps he was never a child.

She moved to the next man in line. "Do you have a wife?"

He remained silent, staring ahead.

"Do you have a daughter?" she asked a third soldier.

"I will kill you myself," he said.

Elissa stood before the line. One of the horses nickered. He was weary, and the headgear was uncomfortable.

"You don't want to do this, do you?" she said to him sympathetically.

"No," said the horse, the one whose rider had promised to kill her. "I hate the noise, the flashing, the squishy things under my hooves."

The other horses tossed their heads in agreement.

"Why don't you just go home?" she asked the horses. "Wouldn't you rather be running free?"

"We would," they said. "But our masters are cruel."

"They strike us with whips."

"And slash our flanks."

"We fear them."

"Don't you fear the battle?" asked Elissa.

"Yes, but we fear our masters more."

"More than the swords? The cries? The blood?" she asked.

"Yes," they whinnied. "We fear our masters more than anything."

Elissa thought for a moment. She knew horses. And there was one thing horses feared more than the cruelty of whips, more than the flash of swords over their heads.

"Wake up," she whispered. "Come out."

The desert was strewn with rocks. Large boulders dotted the hillside, casting their shadows across the soldiers sitting atop their horses. The sun was beginning to set, and the air was starting to cool. For some creatures it was already bedtime.

A small brown head peeked out from under the closest rock. She flicked her tongue.

"Who calls?"

"Come to me," said Elissa.

The snake, curious, slithered out from under the rock. She advanced, winding sideways, in Elissa's direction. A few of the horses spotted the telltale movement past the corners of their blinders and started to dance.

"Come to me." Elissa hissed.

Soon more snakes were sliding out from under the rocks. The horses neighed in terror.

"Snakes!" They pawed the earth and shied, unable with their blinders and headgear to determine the exact location of the snakes. The soldiers raised whips and began to strike the flanks of the horses. This only frightened them further.

"Come to me," cried Elissa.

Dozens and dozens—now hundreds—of snakes had emerged. They seemed to boil out of the ground. Soon there were so many snakes that the desert floor itself seemed to be moving. They slithered through the shadows and through the ranks of horses, toward Elissa, her siren call compelling them forward. By now the horses were frothy with terror. They reared, crashing their hooves down again and again. The horses were screaming. It was a truly horrible sound. Elissa was sorry to cause them such distress. But it would be over soon. They reared and bucked in a frenzy, throwing soldiers into the sky. Those who managed to keep their seats held on for dear life as the horses streaked away across the desert, heading for the hills and freedom.

"Be careful!" Elissa warned the snakes. "Watch for the hooves!"

The snakes converged at Elissa's feet. In a

single writhing mass they swirled around her—a maelstrom of asps and vipers—the deadliest inhabitants of the desert. They flicked their tongues, scenting Elissa.

"What do you desire?" hissed a small asp, twining about Elissa's leg.

Elissa looked down at the slender creature. One strike from his fangs would leave her dead within the hour. She patted his head, unafraid. The little snake closed his eyes happily and wove his body back and forth in the air.

"Nothing more. You can go home now," said Elissa. "Thank you." The snake slithered away. The rest followed, disappearing as silently as they had first appeared. She was very pleased to see not one crushed snake on the ground. And it looked like most of the soldiers had deserted. The soldiers who remained stood like statues, not daring to move. Elissa waited for them to walk away. Then, slowly, they reached down to the ground for their weapons. Elissa watched in utter disbelief. They were simply not going to give up.

"I just don't understand," she said. The soldier nearest her lifted his sword, preparing to strike.

Elissa closed her eyes and took a deep, shuddering breath. There was no point in running. She was surrounded. Then she felt it again. The ground seemed to move beneath her feet. No, it wasn't the ground—it was something under the surface, something that flowed like water. Something that permeated the earth. Elissa recognized the movement, a feeling of deep peace washing over her as the image of light slanting through the tall trees of the hermit's glade leapt into her mind. Once again she experienced the wonderful sense that she was a part of everything around her. With a little shock of delight she realized that the web of interlacing life that was so abundant in the dense forest was right under her feet. Right here in the very heart of desolation, there was burgeoning, bountiful life! In a rush Elissa realized that while individual lives might end, life itself could never be destroyed by the sword. Here was the answer to the question she had not asked, the one the world of men with their conflicts and jealousies and greed had obscured from her. It was not the nature of death she was seeking to understand, but the nature of life.

Elissa felt the web of life beneath her feet: the roots of the trees seeking nourishment. *Come and drink,* she told them. *There is water here.*

The soldier advanced upon the girl, keeping one eye on the ground, wary of snakes. Elissa stood completely still, her eyes shut. The soldier was a little unnerved, but the girl held no weapon in her hand. He raised his sword.

Then something stirred beneath him. He looked down, prepared to cut the snake in half, and there it was! He hacked at it with his sword, but it kept coming, straight out of the ground, wrapping itself around his legs. Within seconds it had wound completely around his torso. He couldn't move. He shouted, but the other soldiers were in the same predicament. Thousands of tendrils pushed themselves up out of the ground, winding themselves with amazing speed around the legs and torsos of the stunned soldiers. In the rear, the remaining soldiers began to break ranks. Snakes could be killed, but there was no defense against this kind of magic. Dropping their weapons, they ran.

Elissa opened her eyes to an astonishing sight. A forest of men stood before her. Unmoving, they held swords in their hands, either by their sides or frozen over their heads, ready to strike. In their eyes was sheer panic. Elissa gave them a reassuring smile. Did they not feel the joy of standing on the earth? The vibrant life encasing them?

The Blue People were arrayed as before. But there were many more of them, several hundred at least. The other tribes had arrived. The expressions on their faces were cautious but not afraid. They had seen a fearsome miracle, but it was their miracle. They fingered their knives, tensed like tigers preparing to spring. The only thing stopping them was Tafat, whose hand was held up in the air. She looked directly at Elissa. But Elissa wasn't ready to give up. The earth had told her something, and she was going to do her best to communicate it.

Elissa turned. She looked into the stunned eyes of the soldier who stood closest to her. His arm, still holding a sword, was raised uncomfortably over his head.

"Wouldn't you like to be a part of the earth?" she asked.

Frantic, the soldier tried to shake his head. The roots tightened. A tendril poked gently at the corner of the soldier's mouth, seeking the promised water.

"Please, dear god, no," he begged.

"Hmm . . ." It was odd that he could not feel the beauty and peace she had just experienced. It was all around him. She tried something else. "You're going to be in that position for a long time," she said. "Or perhaps not." She waved at the Blue People behind her. The expression in the soldier's eyes evolved from fear and shock to pure terror. He struggled to move, which only made the tendrils grasp him even tighter. By Elissa's quick count, two hundred soldiers stood trapped in the thirsty roots of the olive grove. She walked up and down the line, drawing the soldiers' attention to the Blue People, and particularly to their sharp curved knives. She wanted them to be acutely aware of their situation.

"When we let you go," she said, "you are going to put the swords down and never pick them up again."

The soldiers tried to nod.

Then, absurdly, she heard the order to charge.

The soldiers heard it too, but the only body parts they could move were their eyes, which rolled helplessly back and forth like marbles in their heads.

"Whom do you fear more, the Khan or the Blue People?" she asked. It was a rhetorical question, because either way they weren't going anywhere. The Khan, borne aloft by six sweating attendants, hove into view through the dust.

"I command you!" he cried. "Attack!"

When none of the soldiers moved, he screamed in fury.

"What's this? I gave you a command! Kill them!" He advanced. The ranks of immobile soldiers simply did not register in his mind. Then he saw Elissa.

"You!" he cried. "You shall not escape again. Once I have killed them all, I will take you back to my Citadel, where I will make you mine!" He hesitated, the merest pause. "After I have killed everyone else, of course. Traitors, all of them! Even my own mother, blast her!"

Elissa wondered what to say. What indeed *can* you say to a madman? Perhaps all these men were mad. None of them seemed to hear anything.

"Listen very carefully." She spoke slowly, hoping he would understand better than his soldiers had. "You will go away now, or those men over there will kill you. They will carve you into cutlets, and they will fry you. Then they will feed you to their dogs." This was not a threat. Elissa was merely stating the obvious to someone who simply could not see it on his own. "They might not bother frying you," she amended. "Vultures prefer raw meat."

For the first time, the Khan seemed to see the oasis behind Elissa. He pursed his lips and counted Blue People silently. Then he looked at his motionless soldiers. A bead of sweat crawled down his cheek.

"I will give you until the count of ten," continued Elissa. "And then that lady over *there*"—she pointed—"will drop her hand. Do you understand?"

The Khan hesitated only a moment. "Until we meet again," he said. He gave the order to carry him back to the wagon. The attendants obeyed with relief, casting furtive glances behind them as they struggled back up the incline. Elissa watched them squeeze the Khan into the wagon. Watched it sink down. Watched the horses strain and the wheels begin to turn. She counted to ten. Then she turned and nodded.

Tafat's voice rang like a bell in the still desert air. "The prophecy has been fulfilled! The birds have spoken, the earth has moved, and the trees have walked!" She dropped her hand.

To Elissa's profound surprise, the Blue men did not rush forward. She had expected at least an attempt at pursuit on their part. They still held their glittering knives in their hands, at the ready. But instead of running after the Khan, the blue-robed men simply crossed their arms over their chests and laughed, loud and long. The women opened their mouths and laughed with them, not covering their teeth demurely but letting the sound flow unrestrained from their bellies, while the children, at last released from their mothers' restraining arms, hurtled after the Khan's wagon, pelting it with rocks and oranges.

And Elissa's fluttering heart, freeing itself at last from the confines of her body, soared over a desert echoing with the sounds of mirth.

∽ 20 ∽

True Wisdom

The following day the defeat of the Khan was the subject of all conversation in the Great Oasis. The men sat before the cooking fires with their wives, recapping and elaborating on the miracles they had witnessed, while the children dashed through the camp pretending to be birds, snakes, horses, fleeing soldiers. By evening Elissa had been elevated to a minor deity, and her exploits to myth. But Elissa missed it all. She passed the entire day in a profound sleep.

When she woke, it was nearly nightfall. She yawned and sat up.

Maya was sitting on her pallet, eating dates from a bowl. "There's food," she said, pointing a date toward the tent flap.

Elissa turned her head toward the entrance of

the tent, where platters and bowls had been piled. "There certainly is!" she said.

"They've been leaving food all day," said Maya. "I was just waiting for you to wake up."

Elissa helped herself to a bowl of fruit and ate silently. She had a great deal to think about. Maya, uncharacteristically, was also silent. When Elissa looked up from her meal, Maya was gazing at her expectantly.

"Muti told me about the snakes," said Maya. "He said you made the trees grab all the soldiers. Is that true?"

"Mmhmm," said Elissa, her mouth full. Yesterday's experience had been so strange, it all seemed like a dream now that she was chewing on an ordinary piece of bread. But she *had* felt the power of the Earth moving through her as she had easily captured the soldiers. And afterward, she had just as easily let them go again when she saw they could do no harm. All she'd had to do was whisper "Release them," and the roots had slithered back into the earth, leaving not a trace of their passage. And the soldiers, having no wish to repeat their experience, had vanished just as completely.

Maya was quiet, waiting for some explanation.

"I think it was the Healers who really did it, though, with their Lake water," Elissa said finally. But even as she spoke, she realized that what she was saying wasn't precisely true. Whatever force it was that had come up from the ground was of her own making. And while it did not make her afraid, she was uneasy with the thought of such power at her command.

Maya was still looking at her with wide brown eyes. "Do you think he'll stay away?"

"Yes," said Elissa. "I do."

Maya looked a little doubtful. "He is very powerful," said Maya. "What if he gets another army together?"

"That won't be easy," said Elissa. "We really frightened them. And you know how fast word spreads. Besides, he has been made ridiculous. And who wants to follow a ridiculous leader?" Elissa paused. She had learned an important lesson last night, but it was hard to put it into words. "Authority is something that must be granted. As soon as people stop giving it, authority simply disappears. All they have to do is turn their backs. Or laugh."

"Spoken with true wisdom." Tafat entered the tent, followed by Sohar.

Smiling, the two women sat down on the rug, their faces glowing with the satisfaction of a prophecy come to fruition.

Tafat was watching Elissa thoughtfully.

"You have a great deal of wisdom," she said.

"Oh, no!" protested Elissa.

Tafat's metallic eyes glittered. She smiled. "Like it or not, you do," she said. "Fate is not done with you yet. You have something very important ahead of you."

Sohar and Tafat nodded. Apparently this topic had been discussed. Or maybe it had merely been predicted.

Tafat smiled, but she continued to level her gaze at Elissa. Her eyes were filled with a strange mixture of knowledge and regret.

"Sometimes," she said, "wisdom is simply the ability to recognize the truth, and to speak your heart, *in spite of everything you fear to be true.*"

"Isn't that courage?" asked Elissa.

"Yes," said Tafat. "It is wise to have courage."

"And love?" There was a barb in Elissa's heart,

some bit of truth that had lodged there and needed release.

"It is also wise to have love." Tafat leaned over and pressed her lips lightly against Elissa's forehead. "Sohar has news," she said. Then she rose and departed.

"What news?" asked Elissa.

"There is a caravan departing tomorrow for Alhamazar," said Sohar. "You will be leaving at dawn." Sohar raised both hands to one shoulder and twisted the little ring that held her flat-headed pin in place. Her veil fell softly around her arms.

"This fibula will protect you," she said simply.

Elissa examined the pin in her hand for a moment, then hooked it securely through the cloth of her cloak. There was no doubt in her mind that the fibula would guarantee them safe passage with anyone who respected the power of the Ankaa and the sharp knives of the Blue People who protected them. Elissa suspected that Sohar's pin would prove very useful on their journey.

"Take this too." Sohar was holding a little silver vial in her hand. "Use it wisely." Touching her fingers first to her forehead and then to her heart, she turned and left the girls alone.

Elissa held the vial with reverence. There was enough liquid in it to ease the infirmities of several people—or to save one person's life. She drew the little purse from under her robe and slipped the vial inside, next to the shard. Then she tucked the bag back into place. There was no safer place for it.

"We had better rest," said Elissa sensibly. "We have a long trip ahead of us tomorrow." Maya made no objection. She was much better, but she felt as though she could sleep for a thousand years.

The two girls dragged their pallets out of the tent, which was stuffy from the day, and into the cool night air. Within moments Maya was fast asleep. Elissa lay awake for a while, listening to the sounds of drums and voices raised in song. Beneath the palms, the women were dancing, touching their hearts with their fingertips and tossing their heads to cast the evil spirits away. Their dance was joyous, triumphant. It was the victory celebration of the Blue People, the Free People, the ones who knew the ways of the desert and spoke their hearts without fear. They flicked their long, hennaed fingers in the air, dispelling fear and hatred and greed, envy, anger, cruelty, wanton destruction, all the sicknesses of the soul, into the darkness. Bats swooped through the trees, snapping up human frailties, mistaking them for mosquitoes.

As she lay beside Maya, Elissa reflected that their journey might indeed be very long. She had already traveled far since leaving her green valley, farther than she had ever thought she would. The world was proving to be a bigger place than she had imagined, and she had not yet seen the greater part of it. Before her there was another desert to cross, and after that—unknown lands. Elissa's thoughts roamed beyond the desert, past the uncertainties of the journey to come, into the expanding territory of her heart. She looked up into the deep, impassive night sky. To the stars she was nobody—a small girl, hardly more significant than an ant scurrying along, first in one direction, then in another. But unlike the ant, Elissa had a mission. She must learn to speak her heart. And somehow, somewhere, in this great, wide world, she had to find her father.

There was something he needed to tell her.

Erica Verrillo is a world traveler who has studied and worked in a variety of fields, including classical music, Latin American history, linguistics, folk dance, anthropology, refugee aid, and speech communication. She has been a teacher of languages, public speaking, linguistics, and music. She lives in Massachusetts with her two children. *Elissa's Quest* is her first book for young readers—and the first book of the Phoenix Rising trilogy.